"I want you t

Michael's father looked puzzled at the request.

"She's getting introduced to Dani Langston and I don't want her to get the wrong idea." Michael rubbed the back of his neck. "I have nothing to do with the woman."

His father raised a shrewd eyebrow. "You sure about that, son? You know, of the six of you, you're the only bachelor Crawford. Your mother has no one else to concentrate on."

Michael's oldest brother must have overheard. "Is little brother complaining about marriage again?" Joe clapped Michael on the back. "Go ahead and fight it, but you'll find a woman."

"That one looks pretty good," said another brother, pointing at Dani.

"No! She won't do!" Michael turned to face his brothers, and their knowing smiles alarmed him even more. "But…I'm not ready for marriage. You know that, Joe."

"I know that, little brother," Joe said smugly. "But it's Mom you need to convince."

Dear Reader,

April showers are bringing flowers—and a soul-stirring bouquet of dream-come-true stories from Silhouette Romance!

Red Rose needs men! And it's up to Ellie Donahue to put the town-ladies' plans into action—even if it means enticing her secret love to return to his former home. Inspired by classic legends, Myrna Mackenzie's new miniseries, THE BRIDES OF RED ROSE, begins with Ellie's tale, in *The Pied Piper's Bride* (SR #1714).

Bestselling author Judy Christenberry brings you another Wild West story in her FROM THE CIRCLE K miniseries. In *The Last Crawford Bachelor* (SR #1715), lawyer Michael Crawford—the family's last single son—meets his match…and is then forced to live with her on the Circle K!

And this lively bunch of spring stories wouldn't be complete without Teresa Carpenter's *Daddy's Little Memento* (SR #1716). School nurse Samantha Dell reunites her infant nephew with his handsome father, only to learn that if she wants to retain custody then she's got to say, "I do"! And then there's Colleen Faulkner's *Barefoot and Pregnant?* (SR #1717), in which career-woman Elise Montgomery has everything a girl could want—except the man of her dreams. Will she find a husband where she least expects him?

All the best,

Mavis C. Allen
Associate Senior Editor

Please address questions and book requests to:
Silhouette Reader Service
U.S.: 3010 Walden Ave., P.O. Box 1325, Buffalo, NY 14269
Canadian: P.O. Box 609, Fort Erie, Ont. L2A 5X3

The Last Crawford Bachelor

JUDY CHRISTENBERRY

From The Circle K

SILHOUETTE *Romance*®

Published by Silhouette Books

America's Publisher of Contemporary Romance

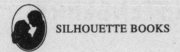 SILHOUETTE BOOKS

ISBN 0-373-19715-2

THE LAST CRAWFORD BACHELOR

Copyright © 2004 by Judy Russell Christenberry

This edition published by arrangement with Harlequin Books S.A.

® and TM are trademarks of Harlequin Books S.A., used under license. Trademarks indicated with ® are registered in the United States Patent and Trademark Office, the Canadian Trade Marks Office and in other countries.

Visit Silhouette at www.eHarlequin.com

Printed in U.S.A.

Books by Judy Christenberry

Silhouette Romance

The Nine-Month Bride #1324
*Marry Me, Kate #1344
*Baby in Her Arms #1350
*A Ring for Cinderella #1356
†Never Let You Go #1453
†The Borrowed Groom #1457
†Cherish the Boss #1463
**Snowbound Sweetheart #1476
Newborn Daddy #1511
When the Lights Went Out… #1547
**Least Likely To Wed #1570
Daddy on the Doorstep #1654
**Beauty & the Beastly Rancher #1678
**The Last Crawford Bachelor #1715

*The Lucky Charm Sisters
†The Circle K Sisters
**From the Circle K

Silhouette Books

The Coltons
The Doctor Delivers

A Colton Family Christmas
 "The Diplomat's Daughter"

Lone Star Country Club
The Last Bachelor

Hush

JUDY CHRISTENBERRY

has been writing romances for fifteen years because she loves happy endings as much as her readers do. She's a bestselling author for Harlequin American Romance, but she has a long love of traditional romances and is delighted to tell a story that brings those elements to the reader. A former high school French teacher, Judy devotes her time to writing. She hopes readers have as much fun reading her stories as she does writing them. She spends her spare time reading, watching her favorite sports teams and keeping track of her two adult daughters.

THE CRAWFORDS

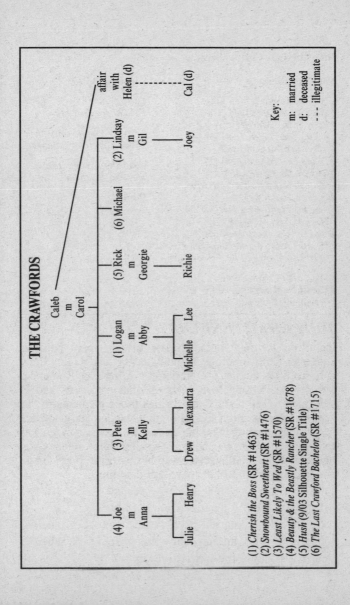

Caleb
m
Carol

affair
with
Helen (d)
----------- Cal (d)

(4) Joe
m
Anna
— Julie
— Henry

(3) Pete
m
Kelly
— Drew
— Alexandra

(1) Logan
m
Abby
— Michelle
— Lee

(5) Rick
Georgie
— Richie

(6) Michael

(2) Lindsay
m
Gil
— Joey

Key:
m: married
d: deceased
- - - illegitimate

(1) *Cherish the Boss* (SR #1463)
(2) *Snowbound Sweetheart* (SR #1476)
(3) *Least Likely To Wed* (SR #1570)
(4) *Beauty & the Beastly Rancher* (SR #1678)
(5) *Hush* (9/03 Silhouette Single Title)
(6) *The Last Crawford Bachelor* (SR #1715)

Chapter One

"Logan, are you sure I won't be in the way?"

Michael Crawford looked at his older brother. Though now twenty-eight and as tall as Logan, he knew Logan still saw him as his kid brother.

"Don't be silly, Mike. How could you get in the way on a ranch the size of the Circle K? Besides, you know that manager's house is empty. I'll help you clean it up, then you can come and go as you please."

Michael looked at the small white frame house one more time. "I appreciate it. This way, I won't miss the family so much since I'll be in the middle of yours."

"True. The kids have already decided you're quite a special uncle," Logan said with a chuckle.

They had just started back toward the main ranch house, where Logan and Abby, his wife, lived, when a car came down the long driveway.

"Guess you've got company," Michael said.

Logan shrugged his big shoulders. "We're not expecting anyone."

The car stopped near them and a beautiful young woman got out. "Excuse me. I'm looking for Mrs. Beulah Kennedy. Is she here?"

Michael knew that Kennedy was Abby's maiden name, but he looked at Logan to answer. After all, he was just a guest.

Logan stared at the slender blond woman. "Who's asking?" he said politely.

"Daniele Langston. I'm a—a family connection."

Logan extended his hand. "I'm Logan Crawford. My wife, Abby, is part of the Kennedy clan. Maybe you'd better come talk to her."

"Would that be all right?" the woman asked.

"Yes, of course. Come with us."

Michael followed his brother and the blonde, wondering what she wanted. Abby and her sisters had inherited the ranch and a lot of money when their elderly great-aunt Beulah Kennedy had died. He figured this Langston woman intended to stake a claim to the inheritance. No doubt she was some scam artist.

He hid the smile he felt coming on. His sister-in-law always accused him of being too cynical because he was an attorney. She could be right. But he reserved the right to wait and see.

They entered the big kitchen, where Abby was setting the table. "I was about to send one of the kids to—" She stopped when she glanced up and saw the stranger. "Oh. Hello. I'm Abby Crawford."

Logan put his arm around his wife. "This is Daniele Langston. She says she's a family connection to Beulah.''

Abby flipped back her long braid and looked at the young woman. ''You are?''

''Yes. I…I wanted to meet Beulah, if that's possible.''

Abby skittered a look at Logan before facing the newcomer again. ''I'm sorry, but Beulah is dead. She passed away over seven years ago.''

Michael watched Ms. Langston carefully, sure she already knew that information. He was amazed to see surprise and sadness in her eyes. Boy, he thought, she was a good actress.

''I see. I'm sorry I bothered you.'' She turned toward the door.

''Wait!'' Abby called out. ''What kind of connection did you have with Beulah? Are you a niece or—''

''She was my grandmother.''

''No, that can't be,'' Abby insisted. ''Beulah had no children. You must have the wrong person.''

''Yes, of course,'' the young woman agreed, and walked to the door. ''I apologize for disturbing you.''

Abby moved toward her. ''Don't go! I'd like to hear why you came here. And I could introduce you to my sisters.''

''I don't want to cause any trouble.'' The woman was still edging toward the door, as if she intended to leave. Michael decided that was a nice touch. She looked the picture of reluctance.

''Nonsense,'' Abby said. ''You must join us for dinner.''

As if on cue their housekeeper came in. "Ellen," Abby said at once, "I've invited this nice lady to join us. Her name is Daniele Langston." She put a hand to her head. "Where are my manners? Daniele, this is Ellen, our housekeeper and the world's best cook." She looked to Ellen. "There'll be plenty of food, right?"

"Yes, of course," Ellen said, her graying blond hair bouncing as she nodded.

"And I want to invite the family over for dessert. Will we have enough?"

"I can make a cake while we're eating," Ellen said. "It'll be ready in no time."

Abby turned back to Daniele. "There, you see? It's no trouble." She smiled warmly. "Now, tell me. Where did you come from?"

"West Texas. I was born and raised in Amarillo." Daniele drew a deep breath and added, "Please, call me Dani."

Abby smiled at her. "Did my husband and brother-in-law introduce themselves?"

"I met your husband," Dani said.

Michael stepped forward and extended his hand. "I'm Michael Crawford."

She put her hand in his, again with reluctance, it seemed. Her smooth skin seemed to burn against his. She was an odd combination of fire and ice.

"Pleased to meet you," she said, and stepped back, withdrawing her hand quickly. Michael made no attempt to hide he was watching her closely. Not even his sister-in-law's obvious hospitality deterred him.

"I'm going to call my sisters," Abby said. Then

she turned to Logan. "Honey, would you corral the kids and make sure they're washed up?" Taking her husband's agreement for granted, she hurried out of the kitchen.

Michael realized he needed to seize the opportunity to warn Abby. Once again she was far too friendly for her own good. "Excuse me," he said to Ellen and Dani and hurried after his brother's wife.

Knocking on the office door, he opened it and stuck his head in. Abby was already on the phone, but she waved him in. After she finished her conversation with Melissa, she looked at him. "Is something wrong, Mike?"

"Could be. I'd be careful about taking in strangers who might try to claim some of your inheritance."

Abby laughed. "Cynical Mike! Surely you don't think she's running a scam."

"Why not? She's claiming to be the granddaughter of a woman who never had children. While she couldn't take all of your inheritance, she could be awarded a hefty sum if she can prove anything."

"But, Mike, if she is Beulah's granddaughter, she deserves some of the money."

"Abby! Bite your tongue. Don't give her ammunition."

Abby smiled and shook her head. "I'll be careful, but I don't believe she's a scam artist, Mike."

He held up his hands. "I'm just warning you."

"I appreciate it, but I think everything will be okay. I've got to call Beth now."

Michael withdrew and returned to the kitchen. Ellen was busy mixing up the cake, and Dani was standing at the back door, looking out at the land.

Probably figuring out how much she could inherit, he thought. He stepped closer to her. "Dani, did you drive down from Amarillo?"

"Yes, I did."

"You must be tired. That's a four- or five-hour drive." The Circle K spread was a half hour southwest of Wichita Falls.

"It's not too bad."

"Are you heading back after dinner?"

"No," she said, but added nothing about her plans.

He decided to ask a few more questions, but Logan and his two children entered the kitchen. His daughter, who was a smaller version of her mother, rushed to Michael, holding out her arms. He swung her up into his arms with a laugh. "Well hello there. What have you been up to?"

Mirabelle was four years of age and always in constant motion. "I been painting my wall. Daddy got mad at me."

Michael looked at Logan. He spoiled his daughter rotten, so Michael didn't think Logan had lost his temper with her.

"I didn't yell at you, but Mom's going to be upset with you. She painted your room last year, remember?"

"Yes, but now it's this year," Mirabelle explained patiently.

Michael grinned. He was pretty sure the little girl didn't comprehend a year, but she was smart enough to use it in her argument.

Logan put his toddler son in his high chair and tied a bib around his neck. "Dani, this is our daughter, Mirabelle—or should I say Michaelangelo—and our son, Scotty."

Dani greeted the children with a warm smile, one that startled Michael.

"Hello," Mirabelle said. "Who are you?"

"This is Dani. She's having dinner with us," Logan explained.

Mirabelle turned back to Michael. "But, Uncle Michael, you said *I* was your girlfriend!"

"Of course you are," he assured her, not making the connection for a moment. Then he hurriedly added, "I just met Dani when she came to the ranch looking for someone."

"Oh. Then it's okay," she said to Dani with a nod. "You can stay for dinner."

"Mirabelle!" her father warned. "Mind your manners."

"I said she could stay, Daddy."

"It is not your decision, young lady, and you know it."

With all the grace of a French dancer, Mirabelle shrugged her shoulders and hugged Michael's neck.

"Mirabelle, you need to get in your chair." Logan turned to Ellen. "Where's your husband?"

"He's upstairs. Could you call him?"

"Sure. And I'll find Abby, too. Then we can eat."

The table was set for eight. Michael carried Mirabelle to her seat next to the end of the table where her mother always sat. He assumed the seat next to the little girl and motioned to Dani to take the seat beside him. "Floyd and Ellen like to sit together on the other side of the table by Scotty."

"I see. Thank you," Dani said, and sank gracefully into the chair beside him.

Suddenly the room seemed full as Floyd came in followed by Logan and Abby. They all took their places, and Logan said the prayer before they ate.

After the blessing, Logan introduced Dani to Floyd. He worked the ranch, having met Ellen here when Logan hired him years ago. In time, the platters of food began to be passed around the table. Michael noticed Dani didn't take much of anything. He kept watching her, frowning. Finally he said, "Are you on a diet? Because from where I sit, you don't need to lose weight." He eyed her slender figure.

She looked up, startled, her blue eyes wide. "No, I'm not on a diet."

"She's probably saving herself for the dessert," Abby said, smiling at the woman. "Never mind Michael. There are lots of men in his family. He's the only one unmarried these days, so he's still uncivilized."

"Hey!" Michael complained. "Logan, are you going to let your wife say that about me?"

Logan grinned. "You can't fight the truth. You know our brothers would agree with her."

All four of Michael's brothers had married good women. He'd never argue about that. But just because he wasn't married didn't mean he couldn't handle women. He'd learned from his one sister. In fact, he was used to being on his best behavior around women.

Abby changed the subject. "Dani, have you lived in Amarillo all your life?"

"Except when I went to school. I moved to Lubbock for my education."

"Texas Tech?" Abby asked, naming the large university located in Lubbock.

"Yes."

"That's a good school," Logan said. He added with a grin, "My family all went to OU, but we try to keep that quiet around here." OU was Oklahoma University, a fierce rival of the University of Texas on the football field.

That remark even drew a smile from Dani. But still she said nothing.

They continued with casual conversation throughout the meal. Dani answered any questions addressed to her, but she volunteered nothing about her life.

Michael realized all they knew about her was where she lived and where she went to school. He wanted to know a lot more.

When the meal was over, Ellen began clearing the table. Abby jumped up to help her. Dani, too, began picking up plates and carrying them to the counter next to the dishwasher. Michael picked up his dishes and followed suit. His brother was cleaning up Scotty so he could get down from his high chair. Then he took Mirabelle to the bathroom to wash up.

"Are your sisters bringing the little ones?" Logan asked as he came back into the kitchen with his daughter.

"No, I don't think so," Abby said over her shoulder as she rinsed a platter.

"Okay, then, come on, Mirabelle. I'll go put on a video, and you and Scotty can watch it while you have some ice cream."

"Chocolate," Mirabelle insisted.

"Sure." Logan got out the ice cream and dished up two bowls of it. Then he grabbed a couple of towels and told the children to follow him.

Michael figured it was the ice cream, Scotty's favorite treat, that had the little boy chasing after his dad. He followed the trio, figuring Logan might need some help. Besides, he wasn't sure he should stay for the dessert party.

After both children were settled in front of the TV, towels tied around their necks, eating their ice cream, he asked Logan if the rest of the evening was just family.

"What if it is? You're family."

"Not Beulah's family."

"I'm not Beulah's family, either." Logan clapped his brother on the back. "Come on. The dessert Ellen's making is great. You'll love it."

They both headed back to the kitchen.

There'd never been a Crawford brother who could resist cake.

Helping clear the table made Dani feel less awkward. She liked Abby and Ellen. In fact, everyone had been very welcoming, except perhaps Logan's brother. Sure, he was handsome, dark and muscular. And he'd been nice, but his eyes gave him away. She glanced up at him, and yet again he was looking at her, gauging her. She knew he didn't think she was being truthful.

It didn't matter what he thought, she told herself. She just wanted to know something about her grandmother. That was all she wanted.

A knock on the screen door interrupted her thoughts. Abby hurried over and opened it, and a young woman looking much like Abby came in, followed by a good-looking, strapping man. Abby turned to Dani.

"This is my youngest sister, Beth, and her husband, Jed."

Dani stepped forward and shook their hands cordially, but she said nothing. She really didn't know if any of them would talk to her about Beulah at all, since they didn't believe Beulah had had any children.

"Oh, here's my other sister, Melissa, and her husband, Rob. Which means we're all here. Come sit down, everyone." They all took seats around the kitchen table, Dani sitting next to Abby.

"Dani told me she thinks Aunt Beulah was her grandmother," Abby said.

Dani suspected she'd already told her sisters, because neither they nor their husbands showed any surprise.

Only the youngest sister, Beth, questioned her. "Why do you think that?"

"I found some papers that indicated she was my mother's mother. She gave my mother up for adoption when she was born." Dani felt awkward revealing that information.

"When was your mother born?" Beth asked.

''In 1939,'' Dani said. ''I was born when she was forty, sort of a late surprise, I guess.''

''So you're twenty-five?'' Michael asked.

''Yes.''

Abby gave her the family history. ''Aunt Beulah married our great uncle in 1942. We thought she'd never had a child. Even though our great uncle died in 1970, Beulah took us in when our parents died in a car wreck about twenty years ago.''

''I see. Was she…nice?''

Dani was taken aback when the youngest sister laughed. The other two smiled.

''She was wonderful,'' Beth said. ''A tough old bird.''

''Beth!'' Abby protested.

''She was, Abby, and you know it. But she loved us.''

''What Beth means is Beulah believed it was best to work for everything. She trained us to do the work on the ranch. She said it would be good for us to earn our keep.''

''Oh. So she was mean to you?''

''Never,'' Abby said emphatically. ''She made sure we didn't think we were a burden to her. We got over our misery and sadness fairly quickly because we were too tired when we went to bed to lie awake and think.''

Dani closed her eyes, thinking about what Abby said. Memories of her own past assailed her, and she shook herself free. ''I see.''

''I hope you do,'' Abby said. ''Beulah believed hard work was good for you. And we do, too.'' She smiled at Dani. "Though maybe not to the extreme she did."

"Thank you so much for sharing that with me. I've been...curious about my family."

"So you really think Beulah was your grandmother?" Beth prodded.

"Yes," she said simply, and finally. Then she stood and eyed the sisters. "I appreciate your talking to me. And thank you, Abby, for inviting me to dinner. It was a delight to meet all of you. But now I should leave."

"But you haven't eaten your cake," Ellen pointed out.

"It looks delicious, Ellen, but I think I'd better go." She slipped out onto the porch before anyone could say anything.

Abby jumped up and hurried after her. "Dani? We were shocked by your appearance, but we may be wrong. If Beulah had a child before she married, it's not surprising that she would give the baby up for adoption. Those were different times back then."

"Of course. I don't blame her. I just wanted to know something about her. And in spite of what you said about Beulah, I think you all loved her very much. And she loved you, obviously. I appreciate knowing that."

"Why?"

Dani smiled and leaned over to kiss Abby's cheek. "Never mind. Thanks for inviting me in."

Then she hurried to her car, afraid she'd burst into tears in front of everyone.

Chapter Two

Michael was up early the next morning, but he didn't awaken anyone. The entire household was at the breakfast table when he came down from his temporary room.

Floyd poured him a cup of hot coffee and set it at his place, and soon after, Ellen handed him a plate filled with all his favorites—scrambled eggs, bacon and biscuits.

"Mercy, I'm getting spoiled," he complained with a smile. "This is a great way to start my day."

"Since it's your first day at a new job, that's a good thing," Logan said.

"Yeah. I've heard the caseload is heavy in this office."

He had taken the job of assistant district attorney in Wichita Falls, the nearest large town in the area.

"You know you love it, brother," Logan said. "That's why you started looking around. You didn't have enough to do in Norman.'' Michael had been an A.D.A. in Norman, the town where OU was located, for several years.

"True. With two new attorneys starting today, we can make a dent in the caseload. I don't think the other A.D.A. is as experienced, but he'll be another pair of hands.''

"Do you know the other person they hired?" Abby asked.

"No. I'll meet him today.''

"Well, good luck,'' Abby said as she stood. "I'm going to ride out with the guys to check on the herd in the south pasture. Are you and Floyd going to check the well that's stopped working?" she asked her husband.

"Yeah, but we should be back for lunch.''

"Good, I'll meet you here. Be careful,'' she added as she rounded the table and kissed him goodbye. Then she hurried out the back door.

"It's still hard to believe Abby is a cowboy,'' Michael said, shaking his head.

Logan laughed. "I didn't believe it either when I first met her. But she convinced me pretty quickly.''

Years ago Logan had applied for the job of ranch manager. Michael recalled that Abby hadn't wanted to hire him at first but she had, solely out of necessity. As Logan had put it, it had been a match made in heaven. Michael looked over at his brother. After two kids, Logan was still crazy in love with the woman.

Checking his watch, he told everyone goodbye and headed for his car. He wanted to get to the office a little early for his first day. He'd already been shown to his desk last week.

An hour later he was organizing his workstation when District Attorney Ned Cobb called a meeting to introduce the new A.D.A.s. Michael hurried to the conference room, looking forward to meeting his fellow workers.

As he stepped into the room, he was called over by Ned, a mover and shaker in his midsixties, with slicked-back dark hair sprinkled with silver. "I want to introduce you to our other new attorney, Michael. This is Daniele Langston."

Dani stepped forward, offering him her hand...again.

Dani felt betrayed. Michael Crawford had mentioned nothing about himself last night. All along she'd looked forward to beginning fresh without anyone knowing anything about her past. Now she found herself confronted with a member of the Kennedy family, no matter how remote the connection.

She stuck out her hand, because she had no choice. He stared at her as if he were as displeased as she was. Finally he took her hand and covered the awkwardness with a comment about not expecting such a beautiful woman. The remark did little to impress her.

The D.A. introduced Michael to another attorney Dani had just met, an older man, calm and friendly. He explained that Dick Stanton would be Michael's mentor for the first month.

Ned hadn't offered Dani a mentor. She looked at him curiously, and as if reading her mind, he smiled and said, "And *I* will be your mentor, Dani. It will be a real pleasure to show you the ropes."

Dani froze. She'd heard that tone of voice before. The man thought he had an easy prey.

There was an awkward silence until Ned ordered all the attorneys in the room to sit down around the big conference table. He guided Dani to the seat next to his, giving her a smarmy smile that made her want to lose her breakfast.

She took her seat and discovered it was opposite Michael. The look on his face told her he thought she'd planned the pairings to her advantage.

She glared at him.

"Right, Dani?" Ned said, catching her off guard.

"I'm sorry, Ned. I was trying to remember the names of the people I've met." She gave him a brief smile and paid attention as he explained he'd told them all she was from Texas Tech Law School. "Yes, that's right."

"And Michael, of course, is from Oklahoma. But we'll have no feuding between the two of you even when OU comes to Texas to play football." Ned gave a hearty laugh, and his staff briefly joined in.

Dani looked around the table. She was the only female, and she was beginning to understand why. Call her naive, but in this day and age it hadn't occurred to her that there would be problems for a female lawyer.

She'd wanted so much to connect with her grandmother, she just assumed a nearby job in Wichita Falls would be perfect.

After a brief discussion, Ned sent them all on their

way—except for Dani. She grabbed the opportunity to showcase her initiative. ''I'd appreciate it, Ned, if you'd give me some time to study the files on the active cases at the moment. Then I might be able to help out.''

''Why, no, Dani, I have no intention of throwing you to these wolves. I'm working on the most important case, and I could use a good researcher. Come along to my office.''

Michael actually felt sympathy for Dani as she followed the D.A. out of the conference room. Ned Cobb was easy to read. He was acting like a three-year-old with a new puppy.

He stepped up beside Dick. ''Has this happened before?''

''New people?''

Michael gave him a knowing look. ''New woman.''

Dick sighed. ''Yeah. She won't last long unless she plays along.''

''He's not married?''

''Sure he is. For forty years. A sweet, gentle lady. But he's our boss. There's nothing we can do.''

Michael didn't like Dick's attitude. The Crawford family tradition said a woman in trouble should be helped. But did he necessarily think Dani was a young innocent?

He dived into the files, enjoying the cases he worked on. He hadn't yet been given his own case, but, after all, it was his first day. A first day that, all things considered, had gone quite well.

When he joined his family later at the dinner table, Abby wanted to know how it went.

"Fine. I'm going to be busy."

"Beulah would tell you that's best," Abby said with a chuckle.

That remark made him feel guilty for not mentioning Dani, but he kept his silence.

Halfway through the meal, Abby said, "I tried to call Dani today, but I couldn't find a listing in either Lubbock or Amarillo."

"Sorry, hon," Logan said. "Maybe she'll contact you again."

"I doubt she'll make the drive from Amarillo after—"

Michael couldn't stand it any longer. He interrupted them. "She's here."

Abby's eyes widened. "She is? At the ranch?" She started up from her chair.

"No, Abby, I didn't mean she's here at the ranch. She's here in Wichita Falls."

"How do you know that, Michael?" Logan asked.

"She's the other new A.D.A. at the office."

Abby looked horrified. "Why didn't you tell us? We could've asked her here for dinner after her first day."

"I didn't tell you, Abby, because I'm still not sure she's not trying to pull a scam on you." He stuck his stubborn chin out, ready to argue with her.

"After reminding us how an attorney is an officer of the court, Michael?" Abby asked slowly. "You said nothing would be worth wasting those three years in law school."

"Yeah, well, it might happen in some cases."

"How interesting," Abby said thoughtfully. "Dani has a law degree, like you. How is she settling in?"

Michael started to tell her Dani wouldn't be around long, but he didn't. Maybe Dick didn't know what he was talking about, or maybe Dani would have no problem cooperating. He didn't know. "Fine."

"Good. I'll call her tomorrow."

Michael said nothing at all. He knew it would do no good.

Dani appreciated Abby's phone call the next morning. It was one friendly moment to count against the hours spent in Ned Cobb's company. But she didn't accept her invitation to have dinner at the ranch.

"How are you settling in?" Abby asked. "If you need any help, I'm sure Michael would help you at the office. Did you find a place to live?"

"Not yet. I'm holding out for the right one," she confessed to Abby, hoping that would stop the questions.

Abby agreed with her attitude, making her feel bad for lying. But she couldn't admit that she didn't think she'd be able to stay, so she didn't want to sign a lease.

When Abby called on Friday to extend another invitation, she was harder to resist.

"Have you found a place to stay yet?"

Initially Dani hadn't intended to tell anyone she was going to stay at the hotel. Unfortunately, Ned had found out about her quarters. He'd shown up last night about nine with a bottle of wine in his arms, wanting to "talk."

She never answered his knock. Nor did she answer his call when the phone rang a few minutes later.

"Um, I've decided to stay at the hotel—"

"Oh, no!" Abby interrupted. "That's impossible. We have a spare bedroom. You'll stay with us."

"No, Abby, I can't do that," Dani said, even as she recognized it as a perfect answer to her problem. But she didn't know Abby and it wouldn't be fair to ask the woman to shoulder her problems.

"Would you at least come out Saturday? We're having a workday with everyone pitching in. We could use some extra hands. We'll swap a good lunch for all your help."

That sounded so appealing. She'd made no friends because the men in the office were standoffish, understandable under the circumstances. And one didn't make friends in a hotel.

"Could I really be of some help?" she asked.

"Oh, yes. It's not skilled jobs. We're talking cleaning and maybe some painting."

"All right. What time Saturday morning?"

"Anytime it's convenient," Abby told her.

When she hung up the phone, Ned entered her office. "Was that a personal call?"

"Yes, it was." She didn't apologize. She already knew he'd use any excuse to put her on the defensive.

"I've been waiting for you to be free. We're going to lunch today with one of the top defense lawyers in the city. I'm sure you'll like him."

Dani was sure the man would cancel and Ned

wouldn't tell her until they'd reached the restaurant. He'd already done that once this week.

"I appreciate the invitation, but I'm afraid I can't do that. I already accepted an invitation to lunch." She didn't explain it was for lunch on Saturday.

Ned stiffened. "In the future, you should clear your invitations with my schedule before you accept."

"Oh, I'm sorry. I thought an hour for lunch was part of my job."

Ned put his hands on her desk and leaned toward her. "Don't get sassy with me, Ms. Langston. You won't have a job if you don't cooperate."

"I have every intention of cooperating, Ned. About work. But I do not intend to have a personal relationship with you."

He glared at her. "We'll see about that."

She leaned back in her chair, drawing a deep breath as he stormed out of her office. So much for her new job. Her fingers shook as she carefully straightened every piece of paper on her desk. Good thing she hadn't found a place to live.

After a moment she got up and went to the law library they had on the premises. She hadn't so much as smelled a legal question this entire week, much less actually worked on anything.

"There's got to be a good case for this, but I can't think of one," Dick Stanton was saying. He and Michael were sitting at a table in the law library, open books scattered around them.

Michael suggested several cases.

Dick said no, he didn't think they were right.

Dani stepped forward. "There's a case one of my

law professors argued a couple of years ago. I think it'd help if I can find it.''

Dick and Michael both seemed doubtful, but they nodded. She scanned the shelves, pulled down a recent book and turned right to the case. She'd never forget it. Her professor had spent an entire week on this one case because of his star appearance.

After reading the case, Dick looked at her with more respect. "Thanks, Dani. This is perfect.''

"Yeah, thanks,'' Michael offered.

She shrugged her shoulders. She knew not to make too much of their appreciation.

"Are you looking up something for Ned?'' Dick asked.

"No, I think he's going out to lunch.''

Dick laughed. "Oh. Then you'll be free for two or three hours. Want to do some work?''

"I'd love to,'' she agreed, enthusiasm coloring her voice.

"This is a sexual harassment case and we could use the female perspective.''

How ironic. She was about ready to file suit against Ned. Maybe she'd put together her own case while she worked on theirs.

She spent the afternoon in the library, looking up cases and discussing issues with the two men. It was the first enjoyable hours she'd had at work.

Ned stepped in a few hours later and told her to come along to his office. The anger in his voice warned her it would be even more unpleasant than usual.

Michael hurried to her defense. ''Dani's being very

helpful to us. You know, you need a female perspective for these harassment suits. Could we borrow her for a little longer?''

Ned's anger rose. ''Yes, fine. Use her for the rest of the day!'' Then he stormed out of the library.

No one spoke or moved for what seemed an eternity.

Finally Michael said, ''Believe it or not, I was only trying to help.''

''And I appreciate it. Do you mind if I stay?'' she asked Dick.

''I don't mind, but you might not have a job on Monday morning. He's rather difficult that way.''

''Then maybe I'll file a harassment suit against him.''

Dick looked alarmed. He excused himself and followed Ned out of the room.

''Careful about throwing out threats,'' Michael warned. ''You're not exactly in a position of strength.''

''How do you know?''

''Just because the guy is making life easy for you, it doesn't mean he's harassing you.''

''Why, thank you; o learned comrade. I'm glad you understand my position so well.'' She began to put away the law books she'd been using.

''Not interested in good, hard work?''

As much as she hated to admit it, he'd pointed out an important fact. This was the first work she'd been given in the entire week. If she threw a tantrum and ran away, she would never establish herself here. She quietly opened the books again and began writing on her legal pad.

When Dick came back, he seemed nervous, watching Dani out of the corner of his eye. She continued to work quietly, addressing any comments or questions she had to Michael. He gradually relaxed again.

When the afternoon ended, Dick actually thanked her for her hard work. "I'm not sure Michael and I could've gotten this far alone. We go to trial on Tuesday. Could you help us prep our witness on Monday?"

"I'd be delighted to."

"Ned said you could work with us. It's an election year and he said it would look good to win a harassment suit."

Dani smiled, glad to understand what was going on. "Yes, I guess it would, to win the female vote."

"Uh, yes. Well, good working with you. See you Monday." He got up and started out of the room. Then he paused. "Coming, Michael?"

"Yeah, I'll be right there."

After Dick had left the room, Michael whispered, "Don't let this go to your head."

Then he was gone.

Dani stared after him. What did he mean? The compliment from Dick? The success in avoiding Ned? She didn't know. But she was enjoying the moment, whatever Mr. Michael Crawford thought!

Chapter Three

Michael planned to work all day Saturday on the manager's house. The place hadn't been used since Rob lived there when he'd first arrived at the Circle K before he married Abby's sister Melissa. When he came down to breakfast Saturday morning, Michael was joined by Logan wearing old jeans and a shirt with paint splotches on them.

"Gee, bro, I don't know how much use you'll be if you put that much paint on yourself," he teased.

Abby walked in at that moment, similarly dressed.

"Abby, you don't need to help us. You must have a dozen things to do," Michael protested, realizing at once that she intended to join in.

"Don't be silly, Michael. Of course I'm going to help. So are Beth and Jed. And our family master carpenter, Rob. Even Melissa's coming to take care of all the kids."

"That's wonderful of everyone, but it's not necessary. I just thought I'd slap on a coat of paint and be done.''

"Absolutely not," Logan said with a sigh. "These ladies go to extremes when they take on a project."

Abby began laying out plans. It seemed Floyd had actually worked as a plumber in his youth and would be installing the new fixtures for the bathroom and the kitchen that Abby had ordered. And Jed had done some electrical work.

Michael stared at her, his mouth open.

"Don't worry," Abby said. "It's to improve the house's value."

He knew better, but he thanked her as if he believed her. What a family! They reminded him a great deal of his own. That was why he enjoyed living here.

Within an hour, they were all working hard. He was taking out some old fixtures when a car pulled into the drive. He recognized it at once. Dani Langston's.

"What's she doing here?" he asked Logan.

"Abby invited her," he said, giving his brother a sharp look. "Is that a problem?"

"No, of course not." What could he say when they were doing all the work for his comfort?

He noticed Dani was dressed casually, also, though she didn't have paint stains on her clothes. As she went past him, with Abby leading the way, she gave him a cool nod of recognition. Nothing more.

He didn't see her for almost an hour until he stuck his head in the kitchen. She and Abby were laying a new linoleum floor.

"Whoa! That looks great!" he exclaimed. "I didn't know you were going to all this trouble."

"We're having a good time." Abby looked at Dani, who nodded in agreement.

"Well," Michael said, not sure what to say. But then he remembered why he was there. "Logan said to tell you he's getting hungry. Hard to believe after that big breakfast, but he insisted I tell you that."

"Oh, wonderful! Come on, Dani. I'll explain." Abby jumped to her feet and caught Dani's arm, pulling her after her.

Michael stood there, his hands on his hips, wondering what that was all about. Then he admired the floor. The old flooring had been nothing but thin sheets of linoleum dating back to the original structure from thirty years ago.

He heard a car honking and wandered back to the living room where he and Logan had been painting. He suddenly understood the message Logan had sent. The entire Crawford family had descended upon the Circle K.

Though it was only a two-hour drive from the Crawford ranch near Lawton, Oklahoma, Michael hadn't considered that his family might come down for the day. Abby, however, had called and made arrangements. Now she was organizing picnic tables under several shade trees. He could see his mother and sister and his sisters-in-law carrying big bowls and plates into the house.

The door to the ranch house burst open again, and this time a herd of kids, led by Mirabelle, ran out screaming and cheering. The group swelled as his nieces and nephews joined them.

"Abby planned all this?" Michael asked Logan as they joined their brothers, father and Michael's sister Lindsay's husband, Gil, and his manager, who had married the mother-in-law of brother Pete. They never bothered with the exact relationship. They were all family.

Suddenly he saw his mother talking to Dani. He recognized immediately what the result of that talk would be. "Uh, Dad, can I talk to you for a minute?"

Caleb Crawford was a big man, robust and active though he was approaching sixty. "Sure. Anything wrong?"

"I want you to warn Mom," he whispered as they walked away from the others.

"Warn Mom? Why? Is someone going to hurt her?" Caleb was instantly on the defensive. His family was his main business, and his job was to protect them.

"No, Dad, nothing like that, but…Abby is introducing Dani Langston to her. We're both A.D.A.s at the office and Mom's going to think she's here because of me." Michael rubbed the back of his neck. "But it's really because Abby thinks she might be kin to them. I have nothing to do with her. Will you tell Mom that?"

Caleb raised one eyebrow. "You sure about that? After all, you work together."

"Not really. She's working with…another group in the office. Just explain it to Mom. Otherwise she'll think— Well, you know what she'll think."

Caleb grinned. "Well, of five sons and one daughter you are the only one not married. She doesn't have anyone else to concentrate on.''

"I need to build my reputation as an attorney before I take on that job. Wives take a lot of work in our family.''

"Shame on you, Michael, saying such a thing about your sisters-in-law.''

Joe, his oldest brother, must've caught his father's words. "Is little brother complaining about our wives?''

"No, Joe, not at all. I just said wives take a lot of time, and I work long hours.'' Michael grinned at him, but he kept his eye on Joe. He didn't want his brother angry with him.

Joe grinned in return. "Go ahead and fight it as much as you want. Mom's not going to rest until she's found you a wife.''

"That one looks pretty good,'' Pete said. "The one talking to Mom now.''

"No! She won't do!'' Michael turned to face his brothers.

The knowing smiles on their faces alarmed him even more. "You tell Mom it's too soon. I'm not even thirty yet. Joe, you were past thirty-five before you married, remember?''

"I remember, little brother,'' Joe said. "It's Mom you need to convince, not me.''

"I think it's so nice that Mike has a friend at work. Sometimes he works long hours. At least he can let off a little steam with someone he knows.''

Dani couldn't hold back a grin. Michael would be

furious if he could hear his mother. Too bad they really weren't good friends. She could use one.

"Well, I think it's so nice that all of your family came today just to help Michael get settled."

"Your family didn't help you?" Carol Crawford asked, sympathy in her voice.

Dani smiled. "No. I don't have any family. I managed on my own."

"Michael will have to bring you home for Thanksgiving. And Christmas. I'll go talk to him about it right now."

"No!" Dani exclaimed. She'd been thinking about Michael's reaction and enjoying those devilish thoughts. But Mrs. Crawford was serious. "No, Carol, you can't. You see, Michael and I really aren't friends. It's because I came to Abby's house to find out about my grandmother and then we accidentally discovered we both worked at the D.A.'s office. That's all. Nothing more."

"That doesn't mean you can't come for Thanksgiving or Christmas. You certainly wouldn't be the first woman Michael has brought home. I know that doesn't mean he'll marry you. But I say—"

"What's up, Carol?" Abby asked as she approached them.

"I want to have Mike invite Dani to Thanksgiving and Christmas. She doesn't have any family at all. I know it doesn't mean they'll marry, but she shouldn't be alone."

Abby looked at Dani's anxious expression. "I think Mike makes Dani uncomfortable, Carol. Besides, she won't be alone. She'll be celebrating here with us."

Dani hadn't expected that turn of events. She almost burst into tears. She hurriedly rushed to the kitchen, under the guise of helping Ellen.

"Oh, my," Carol whispered. "Did I upset her?"

"No," Abby said with a sigh. "I think I did. I hadn't discussed holidays with her. But the more I think about it, I think she may be telling the truth about Beulah. I'm going to visit some of the older members of the community and see what they have to say."

"And she and Michael?" Carol asked anxiously.

"They aren't really at ease with each other." Abby ducked her head and then smiled at her mother-in-law. "I'd like for them to get together, but it can't be forced."

"I know. And I'm so glad you're keeping an eye on Michael. I worry about him, but at least he has you and Logan."

"We're delighted to have him, except for one thing."

Carol grew alarmed. "Michael's not behaving?"

Abby hugged her. "Of course he is. But he's spoiling Mirabelle rotten!" She grinned to let Carol know she was teasing.

Carol sighed with relief. "Well, you can hardly blame him. Mirabelle is such a darling!"

Abby smiled. "And you are the best grandmother I've ever seen."

They went into the house, arm in arm.

With the combined Crawfords and Kennedys, lunch was a great family affair. Michael enjoyed it, even while purposely avoiding Dani. By then, his survival instincts had kicked in big-time, and he didn't want to give his mother any reason to believe he was interested in Dani.

He definitely was not. For all he knew not only was she trying to pull the proverbial wool over Abby's eyes, she was leading Ned on, promising him things she shouldn't. Not the kind of mother he'd want for his kids...when he had them years down the road.

After lunch everyone went back to the manager's house and began projects. They worked steadily all afternoon, and by the time they sat down to leftovers for supper, once again gathering at the picnic tables, Michael had a nice place to live in. He thanked everyone, even Dani. He hadn't intended to disturb everyone's day to such an extent.

"Dani, it was kind of you to come help," he said, trying to sound at ease. But he was sure he failed.

"It was my pleasure. You have a lovely family, Michael. You're a very lucky man."

"Yeah...well, thanks."

She nodded and hurried back toward Abby's house.

So much for trying to be nice. He'd wanted to be friendly, and apparently, he'd scared her. She ran away from him.

After telling his family goodbye, he went to the ranch house to gather his belongings to move into the manager's house. His mother had brought kitchen supplies and linens; all he needed to move was his clothing and shaving things.

He came down from the room he'd been using, followed by Logan with a second load.

Ellen was holding open the door. "Michael," she said, "don't bother cooking breakfast every morning. You'll always be welcome here."

He leaned over and kissed her cheek. "Ellen, you are too good to me, but I'll be here in the morning. Your biscuits are too good to pass up."

Then he walked to his new place and began hanging his clothes in the closet of the master bedroom.

Dani was helping Ellen clean up the kitchen when Michael came through on the way to his new home. She couldn't help but be envious. Not only did he have a nice place to live, but he had family all around him.

That was a luxury she'd never had.

When the kitchen was sparkling as usual, Dani began saying goodbye. Ellen assured her she was always welcome at the Circle K, with Floyd backing her up. Logan, too, invited her to come back anytime. Mirabelle begged her not to go.

With tears forming in her eyes, Dani cleared her throat. "Uh, where's Abby? I want to say goodbye."

"She's in the office. Had a phone call. Go on in. She'll want to see you." Logan smiled at her and gave her directions to the office.

She knocked softly on the door, and Abby swung it open. "Oh, Dani, I was just coming to find you. That was Melissa on the phone. She said she forgot to tell you how good you were with their little ones."

"How nice of her. I had so much fun today, Abby. Thank you for including me."

Abby took her arm and pulled her into the office, closing the door behind her. "I'm glad you enjoyed it. You certainly worked like a Trojan."

"Thanks. I really should go now. I don't like to get to the hotel too late."

"Why don't you stay here tonight? We've got a spare bedroom."

"Thanks, Abby, but I'd better go."

Abby shook her head. "You're way too stubborn."

"I guess so," Dani said with a chuckle.

"You know, Dani, I didn't mean to upset you today when I was talking about the holidays. But I meant what I said about you spending them with us."

"I know you did. That's why I almost burst into tears. You're such a kind person, Abby." She reached out and squeezed Abby's hand.

"But we would enjoy having you so much. Everyone loves you. It would be great."

"I may not even be here, Abby. Let's just play it by ear. If I'm still around in November, then we'll talk," Dani said, sure she'd found a way to postpone Abby's kind invitation.

Abby's expression sobered. "Wait a minute. What do you mean you might not be here in November?"

Dani shrugged. "Things aren't going so well at work."

"But…you've only been there a week."

"I know," Dani agreed with a sigh.

"Tell me what's wrong. Maybe I can help you." Abby's voice was soft with care.

"Oh, Abby. I don't expect you to take care of me. I take care of myself. But that's why I haven't looked for a place to live. I realized the first day things weren't going to work out."

"Is it Michael's fault?"

"No. Not at all."

Abby stood there, frustrated. "I don't want you to go away. What if Beulah *is* your grandmother?"

Dani shrugged. "What difference does that make?"

"It means you belong here, with us, as part of the family."

Dani shook her head and walked back toward the door. "No, Abby, that's not what it means and that's not why I came here."

"Why did you come here?" Abby asked, following her to the door and taking her arm. "Come sit and talk to me." She led Dani to the sofa, and they sat side by side.

"The only family member I knew was my mother. She wasn't a nice person. In fact, she was terrible. I was hoping to find a family member I could be proud of. Someone I could tell myself had passed on some positive things to balance out the negative ones." She gave a wry smile to Abby. "And you gave me that, Abby. I'm very grateful."

"Oh, honey, you ask so little," Abby said, shaking her head.

"But then I'm never disappointed."

"Look, let's drive into Wichita Falls and get you a change of clothes so you can spend the night and tomorrow with us, too. Okay?"

Dani wanted to stay there, wrapped in Abby's family, feeling a part of it, even though it might not be true. She certainly wouldn't put it past her mother to make up papers for some scam. "By the time we did that, your babies would be in bed asleep. I don't want to take you away from them."

"That's not a problem. I'll fix that. Wait here."

Dani shook her head as Abby left the office. If she could choose her family, Abby would be at the top of the list. She was a very generous person, along with her sisters. Just knowing Abby made Dani feel good.

The door opened and Abby came in again, beaming. "Okay, I've got it all fixed. Pack some clothes for church in the morning. And jeans for horseback riding."

"Horseback riding? I don't know how to ride!"

"Don't worry. We'll teach you. Oh, I'm going to love having you here even if it's only for a day or two."

"A day, Abby. Tomorrow night I go back to the hotel so I can go to work the next morning…while I still have a job."

When they reached the kitchen, Dani thanked Logan for going with her to the hotel.

"Oh, it's not me, Dani. I would but Michael insisted on going because I promised Scotty I'd give him his bath tonight."

Surprised, Dani stared at Logan. Then she began protesting. "No, that's not necessary. I can manage on my own. I can—"

The back door opened and Michael entered. "Are you ready, Dani?"

Now she regretted accepting Abby's invitation. Even the short drive to Wichita Falls was too long for her to be alone in a car with Michael. He made her nervous, uncomfortable. "Look, Michael, I can go by myself. There's no need to bother you on your first night in your new house." That sounded like a reasonable excuse to her.

He ignored her remark. "It's getting late. I'll drive." He held the door open and waited.

Abby stepped forward and kissed Dani's cheek. "We'll get the kids in bed and have some more of Carol's cake when you get back."

Feeling as if she had no choice, she followed Michael out into the growing darkness. When they reached his car, she made a last-ditch effort. "I can take my car and be back within the hour. Abby would never know."

"I promised her. She spent all day trying to make things better for me. A drive into town isn't that big a deal. Get in."

With a sigh, she did so. She sat silently as he pulled out on the road, unable to think of anything to say. However, since he didn't speak, either, Dani decided Michael preferred the silence.

"Where are you staying?" he finally asked as they reached the outskirts of Wichita Falls. She named the hotel and gave him brief directions.

"Why haven't you looked for a place to live?" he asked.

She gave him a disgusted look. "Surely you know the answer to that."

He frowned even more. "Why would I know that?"

"Everyone else knows. That's why none of the other employees associate with me. I even get sympathetic looks from the secretaries, but they don't want anything to do with me, either. They've all figured out that I won't be around very long."

"You think Ned is going to fire you? Aren't you pleasing him?"

Dani was astounded by his question. And angered. "No! I'm not putting out! I've refused him at every turn. That's why he's so angry with me."

"Wait a minute! I didn't— I meant with your work!"

Seething, she said nothing.

"Dani, really, I wasn't asking— That's none of my business. I thought maybe your legal skills—"

"Did you find them lacking yesterday, when I worked with you and Dick?"

"Of course not! You were a great help. Dick said you were."

"And did you notice how angry Ned was?"

Michael stopped at a red light and turned to stare at her. "He was angry, but that doesn't mean he'll fire you. You're probably reading into things. Taking things the wrong way."

Dani clamped her lips together, determined not to discuss his supposition. If she did, she feared she'd lose control. She might even cry. And she was determined not to do so in front of Michael.

He pulled his car into the hotel lot. Parking in the first open space, he shut the engine and opened his door, which, of course, turned on the interior light.

Just as Dani opened her door, she saw her boss in the lot. Instantly she closed the door and ducked down. "Shut the door!" she hissed to Michael who was standing with his driver door open.

Michael just stared in at her, looking confused, and she reached over and grabbed the door from his hand, shutting it to turn off the dome light.

"Crawford?" Ned Cobb called in surprise as he came even with the car. "Are you staying here?"

"No, sir. I'm staying with my family outside of town. I'm—I'm visiting some friends traveling through."

He stared at his boss. He didn't ask the obvious question, particularly since the man was carrying a bottle of wine. But he waited.

"I'm trying to keep a particular employee happy," Ned said, giving him an exaggerated wink. "These young women can be so demanding." He smiled, obviously not minding the chore. Then, with a wave, he moved toward the entrance to the hotel.

Michael opened the door and slid back inside as Dani slowly sat up. "You didn't tell me you were expecting company."

She glared at him. "I wasn't *expecting* company. It's the second time he's shown up with a bottle of wine!"

"What happened the first time?"

It was none of Michael's business, but she didn't want anyone to think she'd invited Ned to her hotel room. "I looked through the peephole. Then I pretended I wasn't in."

"So he went away?"

"Yes. And I went down to the desk and demanded to know how he got my room number. Then I changed rooms and told them I'd sue if he got it again."

"He's being that blatant about what he wants?"

"Oh, that's not all. He takes me to long lunches where we're supposedly meeting someone and then they never show up. He drinks and becomes very...friendly. I let him drive me back to the office only once. After that I pretended to go to the rest room and I called a taxi. The third time, I told him I already had plans for lunch. That was Friday."

After a moment Michael said, "I owe you an apology, Dani. I didn't think he'd be that dumb. Are you going to sue him for sexual harassment?"

"No. I'd never get another job. I wanted— I'm a good attorney, Michael. All I wanted was a chance to show what I can do. I should've suspected something of the sort when he hired me, knowing I had no experience."

"So what do we do now?"

"I'm going to make sure they don't give him my room number! But you'd better wait here. I don't want to cause you any problems."

She got out of the car only to find Michael beside her.

"I wasn't raised to hide when trouble was coming. I'll go with you." He started toward the door.

Dani grabbed his arm to stop him. "Michael, I appreciate your offer, but there's no need."

"Yes, there is. Come on."

When they entered the hotel lobby, Ned was standing at the front desk, talking to the clerk. Squaring her jaw, Dani stepped to the side of the lobby, within earshot of the desk.

"I'm her boss," she heard Ned say. "She asked me to drop by. So if you'll just give me her room number, I'll scoot upstairs and drop off my little gift."

The clerk shook his head. "No, sir. I can't. We've promised not to give out her room number. I'll be glad to send up the wine with a note."

"Oh. Oh, of course. That will be fine." He took a piece of paper and wrote something. Then he stood, waiting for the bellhop to take the bottle and note. After thanking the clerk, he made no attempt to hide the fact that he was following the bellhop.

The clerk didn't even notice that Dani and Michael had stepped up to the desk. Until Dani asked for his supervisor.

"I beg your pardon? Is something wrong?"

"Yes. You just provided a guide to my room."

"I don't— Oh, Ms. Langston. We can't refuse to accept gifts to be delivered. We have no policy against that. I didn't think—"

"Your supervisor, please," Dani said, her expression hard and unyielding.

"Yes, ma'am."

The man scurried through a door.

"Good job," Michael said quietly. "Ned *and* the

hotel deserve it.'' He shook his head. ''Ned didn't even try to hide what he was doing.''

The desk clerk returned with an older man who introduced himself as the manager. Dani briefly and concisely explained her complaint. Then she requested her bill be prepared. As soon as she packed, she'd be down to settle up.

The manager tried to argue with her. She gave him an icy stare. ''There will be no discussion. Not only will I take you to court, but I'll also publicly denounce the security you provide for your customers.''

The man began to apologize, but she ignored him, stalking to the elevator.

Michael caught up with Dani just before the elevator doors closed. He'd been standing there admiring her behavior and had forgotten to follow.

''I hope you don't mind giving me a ride to another hotel,'' she told him. ''I think there's one not too far away.''

''I'll be glad to take you there tomorrow. You're supposed to go back to the ranch tonight. Why pay for another room you won't use?''

''Because Abby might think I've got intentions to stay, and I'm not!''

''I know that. Let's get your things. Do you think Ned will still be up there?''

''I hope not. But if he is, I suppose I can resign my job now and save myself the trouble of being fired next week.''

''You don't want to do that. If you leave this quickly, it will look bad on your résumé.''

"It can't be helped," she said, her voice dispirited.

When the elevator doors opened, they both could hear Ned arguing with the bellhop, trying to persuade the man to open the door for him.

"I know how to get you out of trouble," Michael whispered, realizing what an impossible position Dani was in. "Play along," he whispered again as he slid his arm around her waist.

Chapter Four

Before she could speak, he bent over and kissed her lips. "Come on, Dani. I told Abby we'd be back soon."

Dani was still wide-eyed as he tugged her along.

"Oh. Hello again, Ned," he called out as they approached his boss and the bellhop. "I didn't expect to see you again. Dani and I have to pick up something from her room before we go. Where's your key, honey?"

She held it out to him without a word.

He opened the door and then gently ushered her inside. "You grab what you need. I'll chat with Ned."

That must've pleased her since she went in and closed the door behind her.

"I didn't see Dani with you when we met in the parking lot," Ned accused, as if Michael had done something wrong.

"She'd dropped her lipstick and was trying to find it. She's such a sweet woman. I can't believe how quickly we've hit it off. I'm thinking this may be the real thing, Ned. Do you have a marriage policy in your office?"

Ned stood there with his mouth open. When he tried to speak, the words didn't make sense. Finally he managed a coherent question. "You and her?"

"That's right. We may call you our cupid for bringing us together. Of course, it's too early to tell anyone. So don't let our secret out."

"No! No, I won't." After staring at Michael for a moment, he grabbed the wine from the bellhop and handed it to Michael. "Congratulations," he murmured. Then he headed down the hall to the elevators.

The bellhop tipped his cap and hurried after him.

After the elevator closed and Michael could be sure they were gone, he knocked on Dani's door.

It opened at once, which surprised him. "How did you know it was me and not Ned?"

"I looked through the peephole."

"Good. I managed to solve your problem, by the way." He presented her with the bottle of wine.

"What do you mean?

He didn't see any happiness on her face. "I convinced our boss we were practically engaged. He won't bother you anymore."

Michael waited for her to thank him. He thought she might even throw her arms around his neck. After that one kiss, he wouldn't mind exploring a little closeness.

Instead, she glared at him. "You what?"

"I told him we'd hit it off and were thinking of getting married. So he'll know it's hands-off from now on." After a moment, when she showed no appreciation, he said, "Isn't that what you wanted? If you keep this job for a while, it will look better on your résumé. You won't always be having to explain why you left after only a week."

"Yes, but it will be impossible to stay if everyone thinks we're...together!"

"It's better than everyone thinking you're sleeping with Ned!" Michael explained, irritated with her orneriness.

"No one thought that!"

"I did!"

Apparently he'd made her very mad. She turned on her heel and started to haphazardly throw clothes into two large bags. The flush on her cheeks deepened, as though steam were rising to the top. But she stayed silent.

When she closed the bags, he picked them up off the bed and carried them to the door. He and Dani were in the elevator before he spoke. "You'd better make sure Ned has gone before you show too much anger toward me. You don't want to be in the same position again."

"Right! Better for everyone to think I'm sleeping with you than with Ned."

"Well, it is!" he shot back. "Hell, I was only trying to help!"

When the elevator door opened, it soothed him a bit that she was hiding her anger. Even though Ned wasn't anywhere to be seen.

When she asked for her bill, the manager, who was still with the clerk, insisted her stay was free. He apologized profusely for any mistakes they'd made and invited her to stay with them again in the future.

She took her receipt, told him thank you and walked away, leaving Michael to carry her bags. Once they were out the front door, she tried to take one of the bags from him.

"I've got them," he told her.

"I know you do, but I'd prefer to do without your help."

"Not now." The words came out in a harsh whisper as his eyes scanned the lot and noticed his boss. "Ned's sitting in his car, watching us." Without warning he dropped the bags, bent over and kissed Dani's soft lips again, this time making it a deeper kiss.

"Don't—don't do that!" she whispered against his mouth.

"Go get in the car and I won't." He pushed the button on the remote to unlock the doors and the trunk. He loaded her bags and then got in beside her. As he started the car, he realized Dani was practically sitting against her door.

"I'm only doing this to convince Ned," he warned before he kissed her again.

"I don't think he's watching anymore."

"Yes, he is. Wave goodbye, like there's nothing wrong."

She actually did so, even though he'd expected her to ignore him.

"Good girl," he murmured as he pulled out onto the street.

"I am not a child!"

"You're right. You're not a child." The headlights of the oncoming cars lit up her face, and he saw her eyes widen as he pointed out, "But you didn't seem to like it when I treated you like a woman."

"Perfect timing," Abby sang out as Michael and Dani entered the Circle K kitchen. Logan jumped up to take one of her bags, and he and Michael left the room.

"I'm not moving in, Abby, I promise. But I had to change hotels, and Michael said I should wait to check in tomorrow and not pay for a night I didn't need."

"He's right. But I don't mind if you move in until you find your own place. I was thinking. Maybe Michael can help you take care of the problem at work," Abby suggested.

"No! I don't want his kind of help." Dani realized she'd answered too vehemently.

"Something happened, didn't it?"

"Never mind. It's nothing." Dani drew a deep breath. "Can I help with anything?" she asked as Abby picked up the coffeepot and creamer.

"Sure. Take the plates to the table." Abby had already cut four pieces of the sinfully rich chocolate cake Carol had made. "I'll pour the coffee."

As they sat down and waited for the two men to come down, Abby kept looking at Dani. "You're sure everything is okay?"

"Yes, of course," she lied. In an attempt to change the subject she asked, "Does Mirabelle know how to ride a horse?"

The question distracted Abby as planned. She told Dani about her daughter's riding lessons. "I really think it's because she expects to be able to ride. All of us ride, so she assumed it would be easy for her. And it was!"

Just then, the two men entered the kitchen.

"It's about time," Abby said with a smile that hovered on her lips until she realized something was wrong. "What is it?"

"Dani didn't tell you?" Michael asked.

"There's no need to," Dani said emphatically. "It has nothing to do with Abby."

"I *knew* something was wrong!" Abby exclaimed. "What is it?"

"The boss was at the hotel with a bottle of wine, trying to find Dani's room." Michael stopped there, for which Dani was grateful.

"But he's married, isn't he?" Abby asked.

Logan walked over and put an arm around his wife. "Honey, don't be naive."

From the look on her face Abby was obviously putting everything together. She turned to Dani. "He's been harassing you, hasn't he?"

Dani drew a deep breath. "Thank you, Abby."

"What for?"

"For assuming I'm innocent," she said with a wobbly smile.

"Well, of course you are. No one would think—"

She stared at Dani's raised chin and Michael's down-cast gaze and said, "Michael, you didn't!"

"Well, hell, Abby, it was hard to believe the man would act like that unless he had some encouragement," Michael explained. "And I apologized and tried to take care of the situation. But Miss Prim and Proper didn't appreciate my efforts."

Dani couldn't hold back any longer. "He thought it would be better for everyone to think I'm sleeping with him instead of Ned!"

As the two of them squared off at each other, Abby looked at Logan and smiled.

"You think that's funny?" Dani asked, hurt in her voice.

Abby hugged her. "No, of course not, though I do agree it's better for you to be sleeping with Michael. But not much."

"What's wrong with it?" Michael demanded.

"What I meant," Abby said carefully, "is that Dani shouldn't have to pretend to be sleeping with anyone, just to keep her job."

"Exactly!" Dani exclaimed in satisfaction that someone finally understood her point.

"Why don't we calm down?" Logan suggested. After he and Michael sat at the table, he continued. "While what Abby said is the way it should be, I'll have to agree with Michael." Both women opened their mouths to argue with him, but he held up a hand. "That's the way it should be. But that's not the reality of it."

Dani slumped in her chair. "I know." Resignation was in her voice. On the way to the ranch she'd realized she had two choices: go along with Michael or quit.

She lifted her gaze to Michael. ''I should thank you. I don't like the pretense, but I'd like to stay at the job for three months, if you don't mind. Then I'll resign and find work somewhere else.''

Her sudden capitulation surprised Michael. He stared at her, not saying anything.

Logan spoke for him. ''That's a good plan, Dani, and I'm sure Michael won't mind.'' He nudged his brother with his elbow.

''Uh, no, of course not. We'll play it by ear.'' Michael took a bite of cake, trying to look natural.

''And since you're only going to stay for three months, then you should stay here with us,'' Abby offered. ''Any lease you sign would be for at least six months.''

''Abby, I can't stay here for three months. I'd be taking advantage of your friendship.''

''No, truly, you wouldn't. I'd love to have you—''

Logan interrupted his wife. ''Actually, you'd be helping us out if you paid rent.''

Abby frowned at her husband, but Dani looked relieved. ''Really?''

''Sure. With rent coming in from both you and Michael, I'll be able to buy that new tractor I need. Remember, Abby? I showed it to you, but I can't justify the expense.''

Abby didn't reply, and Logan named a figure for rent.

Dani felt better, knowing she'd pay her way and not take advantage of their hospitality.

"Are you sure I shouldn't pay more? It was costing me a lot more at the hotel."

"Actually, you should pay less. Michael gets an entire house for that much and you only get one bedroom. Hey, I've got an idea. You and Michael could share the house. That would be fairer. There are two bedrooms and two baths. Then everyone would believe your cover story for sure!"

Again he nudged Michael, who responded with, "Uh, sure. That space is just going to waste."

Dani still seemed unsure of the idea, especially if she'd be living with Michael. Even Abby wasn't jumping on the bandwagon. "It would give you more privacy, I suppose," she said, as if thinking aloud. And Michael would be the perfect gentleman, wouldn't you, Michael?"

"Absolutely," Michael assured her. Then he took another bite of cake, looking as if he was chewing on rubber instead of moist, delicious cake.

"I...I'd like to feel I helped you buy your tractor, Logan, and it would only be for three months." She turned to Michael. "Are you sure you don't mind?" After all, I'd be sharing your space."

"Doesn't matter to me," he said without looking up.

Dani smiled, albeit hesitantly. "All right, then. I'll rent the second bath and bedroom." She bent down and grabbed her purse, pulling out a checkbook. "How much deposit should I give you?"

"We really don't need a deposit, Dani," Logan answered. "Just one month's rent will be fine."

When Dani handed over the check, he carefully

folded it and put it in his shirt pocket. "Now let's eat this cake. It's not often I get Mom's cake. Not that I'm complaining about Ellen's cooking. Her specialty is peach cobbler. Have you eaten her peach cobbler, Dani?"

"No, but I'm sure it's delicious."

Abby stood up. "There's no time to waste," she said, grabbing her husband's plate even as his fork hovered over it. "I think we should go get Dani settled in."

After the women went to get some extra linens, Michael looked at his brother still sitting at the table. "What have you gotten me into?"

"Nothing. You said you weren't using that space. And Abby obviously wants Dani to stay here."

"I know, but...sharing a house with her might be a little too much temptation."

"I got that impression." Logan's grin made Michael want to slug him.

"You did this on purpose, didn't you?" Michael demanded, a touch of disbelief in his voice.

"Why not? The two of you remind me of my first days on the ranch. I'd like you to have the same happiness I've found."

"Damn it, Logan! This isn't a game. We're not interested in each other. She's—she's leaving in three months."

"A lot can happen in three months."

"But not to me. I'm not ready to marry and settle down. Not yet. In five or ten years maybe."

Logan shrugged his shoulders. "Okay, that's up to you. At least we know she'll be safe here."

Abby came back into the kitchen carrying sheets and a blanket. Dani followed with a stack of towels and washcloths.

"Have you brought down Dani's luggage?" she asked.

"We'll get it now," Logan assured her, bending to kiss his wife. "We'll meet you at the house."

The two ladies continued on, making the walk to the manager's house.

After watching them go, Michael turned around. "I guess I need to write you a check."

Logan grinned again. "You know you don't. But Dani needed to feel that she wasn't taking charity. She's never had a family who helped her out. She's had to pay her own way. Must've been hard getting through law school like that."

Michael shook his head. "Yeah. I hadn't thought of that."

"From what we understand, she and her mother didn't get along too well. She told Abby her mother wasn't a nice person."

"That's all right. Mom will adopt her. Her heart's big enough for another child."

Logan chuckled. "Yeah, it is. But Dani won't allow that. Abby told me she's going to ask around about Aunt Beulah. If what Dani claims is true, maybe we can adopt her instead."

"Yeah, well, we'd better get those bags over there before Abby gets upset," Michael said, calling an end to their discussion. He'd had enough talk of Dani

Langston for one night. Already, she was affecting his heart, soliciting sympathy. He'd had such a wonderful life, his actions supported and applauded by his family. He'd always known if he needed help, he only had to ask.

Dani, on the other hand, apparently had to work her way through school, even law school, and continued to make her own way. It made Michael feel she was stronger than he.

When they reached the house with Dani's bags, Abby was already impatient. "I was beginning to think it was time to get out the bull whip."

Logan didn't blink an eye. "No way, sweetheart. We just wanted to give you plenty of time to get the bed made."

"Thanks," Abby said dryly. "Oh, Michael, I forgot to get a pillow for Dani. Can she borrow one of yours for tonight?"

"Sure. I'll go get it." The stark contrast of his bedroom, containing anything anyone could need, compared to the bareness of the other room, struck him. He grabbed the extra pillow and carried it back to Dani.

"Thank you," she said, turning to put the pillow on the bed.

"I've got a spare lamp if you'd like to borrow it, too," Michael offered.

"No, thank you. I'll pick up a lamp when I'm out tomorrow."

After what his brother had said about Dani's solitary existence, Michael didn't take offense at her rejection.

Dani gave Abby a hug and gently pushed her toward the door. "I'll do the unpacking. You go back and put your feet up."

"Are you sure? I don't mind."

"I know you don't. You're the nicest person I've ever met. But I'm sure."

"All right. We'll see you at breakfast in the morning. Come over whenever you get up."

Dani smiled. "I will. Thanks again."

Logan bade them both good-night and took Abby's hand to urge her out the door. "We'll see you tomorrow."

Silence fell as Michael remained in Dani's room. "You're going to be all right?"

She looked up, surprised. "Of course. Thank you for letting me stay at your place, Michael. I'll try not to be any trouble."

He shrugged. "It's not my place. It's ours."

"Well, thank you," she murmured, standing there, waiting for him to leave her room.

"You sure you don't need any help?"

"No, I don't, Michael." She was firm in her response.

With a smile, he said good-night and went to his bedroom. He was tired. All week he'd looked forward to the first night in his new residence. But things had changed. Now Dani was in the next room, with just a thin wall separating them. He wanted to crawl into bed but he knew he was too distracted to sleep.

Then he heard her turn on the shower.

"Oh, great," Michael muttered. Now all he could

think about was her naked, water sluicing down her bare skin.

He went into the living room and turned on the television, hoping to drown out the sound of the shower. He found a baseball game on. Since it was September and near the end of the season, the game was important. Even so, Michael knew the second the shower ended. He imagined Dani's body glistening with drops of water as she rubbed herself dry.

"Hell," he muttered, sitting up and leaning forward to concentrate on the game. If he had to go through this every night, he was going to lose a lot of sleep.

A door closed, indicating Dani had gone back to her bedroom. Now he could relax.

Five minutes later he realized he was desperately concentrating on what he couldn't hear. He was going crazy.

He sprang to his feet and went to the kitchen. Maybe eating would distract him. He opened the refrigerator and found nothing interesting. The pantry had a package of two cupcakes. He grabbed it and opened it.

Two cupcakes.

Maybe he should offer one to Dani. He left the kitchen and tapped on her bedroom door.

"Yes?"

"Uh, I'm having a cupcake. Do you want one?"

The door barely opened and Dani stared at him in disbelief. "After your mother's cake? No, thank you."

"Oh. I just thought I'd share."

"I appreciate the offer, but no, thanks."

He noticed she had on a blue robe, but at the neckline he glimpsed a white lacy material. A sexy nightgown, he guessed.

"How about a glass of wine? We have Ned's gift."

"No, I don't drink wine."

"Why not?"

"My mother was an alcoholic."

So much for casual conversation. "I'm sorry."

"It's all right. You didn't know. I'm going to bed now, Michael. I'll see you in the morning." Without awaiting his reply, she closed the door.

Michael stood there, staring at the two cupcakes in his hands. He went back to the kitchen and dumped both of them in the trash can. Then he returned to his bedroom and undressed for bed. He'd learned one lesson tonight: he was going to have to work harder at his self-discipline if he was going to survive sharing a house with Dani.

Chapter Five

When Michael finally opened his eyes the next morning, he knew he'd overslept for church. After all, he'd lain in his bed, unable to sleep until about four in the morning. Thanks to Dani.

Not resting and now having to rush combined to give him a grouchy attitude.

Also thanks to Dani. Hearing no movement in the house, he assumed Dani had gotten up on time. He jumped in the shower and dressed quickly, then headed over to Abby's house, sure he'd find something to eat.

He did. But he also found Dani. She was at the table finishing breakfast.

"Why didn't you go to church with Abby?" he demanded, not happy to see her sitting all alone.

"Abby told me to come with you because I hadn't had any breakfast. Ellen made it for both of us. Your plate is still in the oven."

Michael hurried to the oven to retrieve his breakfast. "I think we'll be on time for services if I eat in a hurry." He sat across from her and began to scoop up forkfuls of scrambled eggs.

"How was your first night?" he asked between bites.

"It took a while to get to sleep," she said.

He frowned. He could certainly relate to that. "Why?"

"It's a new place. Very quiet."

That hadn't quite been his problem.

They were silent while he finished his breakfast and rinsed their dishes.

"We'll take my car, since I know where the church is," he finally said as they left the house.

The church was only about five minutes away. After they parked and approached the front door, the sound of organ music drifted out to them. Dani scooted inside and Michael followed.

"Abby said they'd save us seats," she whispered, looking for her new friend. "There they are," she said, and started down the aisle just as everyone was sitting down after the hymn.

Michael fell into step behind her, but he was frowning when they reached the row where Abby and Logan were sitting. They'd moved over, but not enough in Michael's mind.

He motioned he'd sit with Jed and Beth in the next row, but Abby grabbed his arm and tugged on him till he sat with them. The small space between Dani and the arm of the bench left him no choice but to press against her. He automatically put his arm around her, enabling him to sit back. "Sorry, there's not enough room."

For an hour, he remained pressed together with Dani, staring at Abby when he could catch her eye. By the time the final prayer was said, he knew he'd purposely been trapped. His grouchiness had turned into downright anger.

He stepped into the aisle and waited until Logan joined him after the ladies had come out. "A bit crowded today, eh?" Michael murmured.

"A little."

"A lot on our row. What's the deal?"

"I don't know what you're talking about," Logan said firmly, hurrying to catch up with his wife.

Michael knew his suspicions had been right. Abby *was* setting him up. He decided he would have to be careful. He'd already put himself in deep trouble, sharing a house with Dani. And, damn it, *he* had made things worse by volunteering to pretend to be her fiancé.

Had Abby planned that trap, too? No, he thought, shaking his head, he'd have to admit his culpability. He'd jumped headfirst into that situation without any encouragement.

Thanks to his brothers.

They'd all been caught, trying to help the woman each of them had been courting. After watching his brothers end up at the altar, he should've known better.

He caught up with the others just in time to discover that Dani had arranged for Logan to ride with him, along with Mirabelle, while she was going in Abby's car.

That irritated him, too. What was wrong with her? Did she hate him? He'd done everything he could for her.

Hold on, he told himself. He didn't want her to like him. Damn! She had him so confused.

"You okay?" Logan asked as they got into Michael's car. He fastened his daughter's seat belt in the back seat and then his own. Then he looked at his brother, who still hadn't answered his question. "Michael?"

"Yeah, I'm fine." Then he shook his head. "Actually, I'm not. You tell Abby to stop trying to get Dani and me together. And you, too."

"What are you talking about?" Logan feigned innocence.

Michael gave him a sharp look. Then he started his car and backed out. "Dani could've gone with y'all to church instead of waiting for me. And it would've been nice to have more than a foot of the pew for both of us. She was practically sitting in my lap."

"And you're complaining about a beautiful woman being close to you? What's wrong with you, boy?" Logan asked, a twinkle in his eye.

"I'm not ready for marriage, Logan. And Dani wouldn't be my choice if I were. I bet she can't bake a pie or cook a meal. And she probably wouldn't want to be off work to have a baby, much less stay home and take care of him."

"Why should she? You're not willing to do that, either," Logan pointed out.

"That's easy for you to say. Abby takes care of everything," Michael replied, still with anger in his voice.

"Abby runs the ranch. And she doesn't do that from the house. She's out early and works hard. Fortunately, we have Ellen to help us, but both of us work hard and take care of our children."

Michael wished he'd kept his mouth shut. "Yeah, but—"

"All our brothers' wives do things besides raise children. Anna is a housewife and mother of three, but she does tons of charity work in the community, like Mom. Kelly and Lindsay have Oklahoma Chic."

"Okay, bro, you've made your point. But the bottom line is I'm not ready to take on a wife and help raise children. That's *my* point. And I don't want any pressure."

Logan raised both hands in a sign of surrender. "No problem. I wouldn't wish anyone resistant to marriage on Dani. She's had enough battles to fight. By the way, Abby is grateful for your helping Dani with the problem at the office."

"I did it because she was in an impossible position. At least I thought she was."

"What do you mean?" Logan asked.

"Maybe she played it that way, secretly encouraging Ned, so I'd fall into her trap."

Logan burst into laughter. "Lord have mercy, Michael, you're more than a little conceited. I'll admit you'll be a good husband someday, but I don't think Dani has to go to such lengths to find a man."

"Thanks for the vote of confidence, brother." Michael turned into the long driveway and parked beside the manager's house.

"You'd better figure out what you want, Michael. You're sending out some contradictory messages," Logan pointed out with a grin. Then he turned to help his daughter out of the car.

"Daddy, does Uncle Mike like Dani?" Mirabelle asked.

"I think he does, but he's not sure." Logan ignored his brother's glare.

"Why?" Mirabelle asked, staring at her uncle.

"Of course I like Dani," Michael admitted. "As a friend."

"That's what I meant," Mirabelle said. "She's my friend, too."

"Good." Michael smiled, but it wasn't genuine. "Let's go help get dinner on the table, okay? I wonder what Ellen is fixing for us today?"

"Fried chicken. And she said I could have the drumstick," Mirabelle announced, wriggling free from her father's hold to begin running to the house.

Michael followed her, but he wasn't in such a rush. God only knew what matchmaking Abby had waiting for him.

"Uncle Michael says he likes you," Mirabelle announced as soon as she caught sight of Dani in the big kitchen.

All three women—Abby, Ellen and Dani—stopped and stared at the child.

Abby broke the silence. "Well, of course he does,

honey." She ushered the child out of the room. "Now I want you to go upstairs and take off your dress and hang it up. Then you can put on jeans and a T-shirt."

"Yes, Mama." Mirabelle dashed up the stairs.

"I wonder what brought that on," Ellen muttered, looking at Dani out of the corner of her eye.

"Who knows," Abby replied. "Mirabelle has big ears and Michael forgets she's around sometimes."

"She probably wanted to know why I'm staying in the manager's house with Michael," Dani said after she cleared her throat.

"I'm sure that's it," Abby agreed. "Oh, I forgot to make the biscuits, Ellen, and I still have to make a salad."

"I'll make them after I finish frying the chicken," Ellen said calmly.

"I could make them, if it would help." Dani's voice was hesitant and Ellen gave her a sharp glance.

"Why, of course it would help," Ellen assured her. "I had no idea you knew how to make biscuits."

"I won't guarantee they'll be as light as yours," Dani said with a smile.

"Don't you worry. They'll do." Ellen got down a bowl from the cabinet and placed it on the counter. "You can work here, child."

As she worked, Dani could feel Ellen's and Abby's eyes on her. But she knew how to make biscuits. She'd been taught by an expert. They'd see soon enough.

Later, when everyone settled around the dinner table, Logan picked up the plate of biscuits and took one, biting into it even as he passed the plate to Floyd. "Hey! Who made the biscuits?"

"What makes you think I didn't?" Ellen demanded.

"Well, no offense, Ellen, but they're better than yours," Logan said with a grin. "And I know they're not Abby's. That's one of the few things she can't make."

Floyd tasted his biscuit and nodded. "He's right. Sorry, honey, but even yours aren't as good as these. They're really light and fluffy."

"I made them," Dani said.

Michael jerked his head up and stared at her. "You did?"

"Yes," Dani said proudly. "Oh, I almost forgot the other pan." She hurried to the oven and pulled out another pan of golden-brown biscuits.

"You planned this!" Michael protested.

Dani stared at him, wondering what he was talking about. He was pointing at his brother.

"No, I didn't," Logan responded calmly. He turned to Dani. "How did you learn to make such good biscuits? I don't think they teach that at law school."

She shook her head. "I took a job as a short-order cook in a café, only I didn't really know how to cook. Because I needed a job so badly the chef took pity on me and taught me how to cook. You should taste my pie crust," she added, smiling at them all.

Ellen was pleased. "Mercy, child, I'm going to have to get you to give me lessons."

"I will, Ellen. Anything I can do to repay your and Abby's kindnesses to me."

Michael stood up, throwing down his napkin, and stomped away from the table, muttering, "I'm not hungry." The screen door slammed behind him as he walked out of the house.

"Did I say something wrong?" Dani asked, staring at the back door.

"Mike can be difficult at times. Just ignore him," Logan said. He couldn't hide a grin, which Dani thought was strange. Then she saw him wink at his wife.

She shrugged it off, figuring whatever was going on between Michael and Logan, they'd work it out. After lunch she told Abby she was going to pick up some things she needed now that she had a place to live.

"Want some company?" Abby asked.

"I'd love some," Dani said, delighted with the idea. She'd spent so much of her life alone. Her joy was compounded when Ellen asked to join them.

As they drove into town, Dani laughed with her two new friends and counted them among her blessings.

Logan knocked on the door of Michael's house. When there was no answer, he let himself in and proceeded to the master bedroom.

He stopped at the closed doors. "Mike?"

He heard movement and waited patiently until the door opened.

"What do you want?" Michael asked.

"I just wondered if you'd gotten your appetite

back. There's some leftovers and the ladies have gone shopping, so you can get something to eat without having to apologize.''

''Yeah. Okay. But I'll apologize when they get back. I just couldn't believe—I thought you'd planned it!''

''Well, I didn't. But I think you underestimated that little lady. She not only managed to put herself through college and law school, but she can cook.''

''That still doesn't mean she's the kind of woman I want to marry. I'm going to do what I can to help her out, but that doesn't mean anything.''

Logan smiled. ''Come on, little brother. There are a couple of biscuits left.''

''Just two? Well, I guess that will have to do.''

''Hey, man, you don't get both of them. I'm taking one!''

They both broke into a run.

Dani had never had such a wonderful shopping trip as that afternoon. She didn't buy a lot, but Abby and Ellen certainly encouraged her. They only protested when she bought groceries.

''But you'll eat with us,'' Ellen insisted.

''No. I usually just have yogurt for breakfast. If I ate your cooking every meal, I'd gain a hundred pounds and have to buy an entire new wardrobe.''

''But the men will want your biscuits,'' Ellen warned her.

''I'll show you how to make them. And I'll join you on Saturday and maybe Sunday.''

When they got back home and stored all Dani's

purchases, the children were up from their naps and Mirabelle was ready to ride her pony. Dani gamely let Abby teach her how to ride a horse.

Even though she soaked in a hot bath that evening, she was still stiff and sore the next morning. She took a hot shower, hoping to ease her discomfort. Still, at breakfast, she ate her yogurt standing up, only leaning gingerly against the kitchen cabinet.

When Michael came out of his bedroom, dressed in his three-piece suit, Dani nodded at him but said nothing. Sure, he'd apologized for his rude behavior yesterday. His words had been fine and right, but she knew he was unhappy with her. She had no choice, however, but to go to work and hope Michael's sacrifice would protect her from Ned.

Michael nodded back. "I'm going on over for breakfast. I'll see you there."

He didn't wait for a response. Obviously he hadn't noticed the yogurt in her hands. Not surprising since he barely looked at her.

She threw away the empty carton and rinsed the spoon before putting it in the dishwasher. Then she gathered her briefcase and headed for her car. In a few minutes Michael would find out that she didn't intend to ride to work with him.

Michael settled in at the breakfast table. When he took a bite of biscuit, he knew Dani had made them. He said nothing, eating steadily.

Floyd patted his slight paunch and smiled at his wife. "Ellen, honey, these are terrific!"

"Thanks, Floyd. It was good of Dani to show me how to make them."

Michael paused, the biscuit halfway to his mouth for a second bite. "Dani didn't make them?"

"No, she showed me how. It would be a bit much for me to ask her to cook for all of us when she's not going to eat with us."

"What do you mean, she's not going to eat with us?" he asked, frowning deeply.

Abby answered. "She usually just eats yogurt for breakfast."

Suddenly suspicious, Michael got up and went to the back door. As he thought, Dani's car was gone. "I thought we'd drive in together to make sure Ned got the right impression."

"Did you discuss that with Dani?" Abby asked.

"No. I'll talk to her at work," he growled before he sat down and finished his breakfast without a word.

On the way into town, he tried to figure out what Dani was doing. He'd apologized for his behavior. Why would she drive into work without him? Did she not want his protection?

That thought should've pleased him. Instead, it irritated him. He'd sacrificed for her. He didn't want the gesture thrown back into his face, as if she didn't need him.

The more he thought about it, the more annoyed he got. By the time he parked his car at the D.A.'s office, he was loaded for bear. He charged in, heading straight for Dani's office.

It was anticlimactic to find it empty.

He turned to Angie, the secretary who served four

lawyers. "Where's Ms. Langston? I saw her car in the parking lot."

"Mr. Cobb asked her to come to his office."

"Damn! Uh, I'll join them," he said, trying to sound as if he was expected. He hurried away before she could stop him.

The door to Ned's office was closed. Feeling he was letting Dani down, he briefly knocked and opened the door. Dani was standing in front of Ned's desk, as if she were being scolded.

"Morning," Michael said abruptly.

"Is there an emergency?" Ned asked, raising his eyebrows.

"No, I thought maybe...maybe you were discussing the harassment suit, but I see Dick isn't here. I was afraid I was late." What else could he say? He stared at Dani, looking for signs of distress.

"Mr. Cobb wanted to know our wedding plans," she said calmly. "I told him we hadn't set a date yet. That I wanted to get in a year's experience before we set up housekeeping. Besides, everything is still very new. He's agreed I can remain at my job until we make a final decision. I was explaining how much I was looking forward to working today on the harassment suit with you and Dick."

Michael nodded, realizing she'd put him in the picture very neatly. "Right. I think having the female perspective will be very helpful."

"Yes," Ned said, pursing his lips together. "Dani says you two can work together as professionals. Is that true?"

"Absolutely."

"Good. Well, let me know how the case progresses."

"Yes, sir." Michael stood back as Dani came toward the door. He held the door open for her and followed her out.

"Why didn't you wait for me?" he asked under his breath when they were out of Ned's earshot.

"I knew you were upset about something. I thought I could handle the situation by myself."

"I keep my word, Dani. From now on, we'll drive to work together."

She waited until she reached her office. Once he followed her in, she gave him her answer. "No, we won't."

"Damn it! It's too late for you to—"

"Morning," Dick said, smiling at them from the doorway. "Ready to go to work?"

Chapter Six

The three lawyers worked together all morning. When they broke for lunch, Michael tried to get Dani alone, but she eluded him and escaped in her car. He muttered under his breath and joined Dick for lunch. After all, she'd given him no choice.

After their orders were brought to their table, Dick said, "Dani is a good lawyer. She's being a big help on this case."

"Yeah," Michael agreed. "But she has an advantage we don't have."

"I know. She's female. I thought she'd be gone within a month, unless she was the kind to cooperate with Ned." Dick gave him a sharp look. "She's a looker, too. But are you sure you're not rushing things?"

"Ah. So Ned spread the word?" Michael asked, even though the answer was obvious.

"Yeah. He told me this morning, just in case I

wanted to make a play for her, he said. He was giving his reason for not being able to reel her in. His ego is monstrous. You're lucky it didn't cost you your job.''

"I'm not a pushover. He couldn't justify firing me after only a week." Michael pressed his lips together. "He shouldn't have been able to justify doing that to Dani. But it is a man's world.''

Dick laughed. "Yes, it is, but since I'm a man, I don't complain too loudly.''

Michael turned his attention to lunch, but his opinion of Dick diminished. Part of Michael's reason for becoming a lawyer was to provide assistance to those who needed it. It seemed Dick was driven by something else.

When they returned to the office, less friendly than when they'd departed, they found Dani at work in the law library.

"Did you have a good lunch?" Michael asked.

"Yes, I did," she said with no elaboration.

He was reminded of her first visit to the ranch. She was everything that was polite, but she revealed nothing about herself. Again his suspicions were aroused.

"Where did you go to lunch?" he asked, lowering his voice as Dick organized his papers.

She watched Dick as she muttered, "It doesn't matter.''

Dick looked up. "Ready? I'll check and let the girls know that we're in here waiting for our witness to arrive." He walked out of the library.

"Why are you so secretive?" Michael demanded, anger in his voice.

"Why are you so curious?" she returned, staring at him with her blue eyes.

"Look, Dani, I've put myself on the line. If you're meeting someone at lunch, I could look like a fool because I tried to help. Is that fair?"

"No. I promise I'm not meeting another man. There, that takes care of your problem. Satisfied?"

"No. I want to know where you went."

Dani drew a deep breath. Finally, she said, "I went to the park with a sandwich."

"By yourself?" Michael asked, frowning.

"Yes, Michael, by myself."

"Why?"

At that moment Dick came back in, followed by a young woman. Michael had no choice but to turn his attention to the harassment suit.

The only heartening thought was that Dani would go home to the house they shared. She couldn't run away from him after work.

Dani had a call late in the afternoon. Worried that it was Ned, she sighed with relief when she recognized Abby's voice.

"I wondered if you had plans for this evening," Abby said in her usually cheerful tone.

"Plans? No, no plans."

"I want us to go to the nursing home and talk to a couple of ladies who knew Beulah most of her life. I thought we might find out more about your mother."

Dani felt her stomach tighten. In a thin voice she tried to dissuade Abby. "That's not necessary. I know about my mother. More than I need to know. And you've told me about Beulah." As much as it hurt, she said, "If you've changed your mind about me living on the ranch, I can understand that. Just—"

"Dani, no! That's not what I meant."

"Then let's just forget my assumption that Beulah is my grandmother. It doesn't matter."

After a moment of silence, Abby agreed. "I'll see you this evening."

Dani hung up the phone, knowing she'd upset Abby. But she'd learned more from asking about Beulah than she'd ever intended. And if Abby was able to prove Beulah was her grandmother, Dani worried that Abby would think she was after some of the Kennedy money.

Abby probably already thought so.

Dani blinked away the tears in her eyes. She couldn't stay on the ranch now. She'd have to move. But she didn't want to leave. They all treated her like family. Being with them was a gift beyond price. But it was slipping away.

Mad at herself for being so weak, she wiped her eyes. She knew better. Life wasn't easy. But this time she'd made the mistake of believing it had a fairy-tale ending.

She wasn't there.

Michael had taken a call in his office close to five o'clock. When he returned to Dick's office, Dani was gone. When Dick said something about her seeming upset, Michael headed home as soon as he could.

Her car wasn't parked where it usually was and the

house was silent. Without hesitation he headed straight for Logan and Abby's house.

As soon as he stepped into the kitchen, he saw Abby working intently on stirring something, with an intensity that made him wonder what was so important about the bowl's ingredients. "Abby?"

Startled, she jerked up and turned, her dark braid whipping around. "Oh, Michael. Home from work?"

"Yeah. Have you seen Dani?"

She turned away, not willing to look at him as she answered. "No. I haven't."

"Did you call her today?"

"Why do you ask?"

Michael didn't know what to say. But he'd done enough cross-examinations to know she was hiding something. He was greatly relieved when Logan entered the house.

Abby ran to her husband. He automatically opened his arms to her and looked at Michael. "What's wrong?"

Abby didn't say anything.

"I'm not sure," Michael said. "I asked Abby if she called Dani this afternoon and she won't answer."

"Michael," Logan said calmly, "my wife is not on the witness stand. She's family. Now what's going on?"

Michael flung himself into one of the chairs at the table, frustrated. "I'm sorry, Abby. But someone called Dani this afternoon and upset her. She slipped away while I took a phone call. When I came back, she'd gone for the day. But she didn't come home."

He rubbed his forehead. "I didn't mean to come on so strong, Abby. I'm just worried about her."

Abby stared at him. Finally, she sat down across from him. "I did call Dani today."

"What about?" Logan asked, sitting down beside her, his arm on the back of her chair.

"I wanted us to go to the nursing home and visit a couple of Beulah's old friends who might be able to tell us whether or not Beulah ever had a child. I thought Dani would want to know the truth."

"What did she say?" Michael asked, leaning forward.

"She said no, and she offered to move out." Abby began blinking rapidly, fighting tears. "I...I didn't know what to say. And I realized Michael's warning about her might be true." She turned to her husband. "Oh, Logan, I don't know what to do. I don't want to suspect her, but—"

"That's a real disappointment," Logan agreed, tightening his embrace.

Michael shoved his chair back and leaped to his feet, pacing around the room. "I don't think Dani is the kind of person who would try to trick you."

"But you're the one who warned me about her," Abby reminded him.

"I know, but...I've worked with her. She's a smart woman. It seems to me she wouldn't handle things like this if she intended to file suit for part of Beulah's estate."

"I can't be sure anymore," Abby confessed. "How can I trust her if I think she's lying about Beulah?"

Logan and Michael exchanged a look. "You can't,

honey," Logan agreed. "I'll talk to her about moving out. I won't have you unhappy."

"Oh, Logan, I don't know!" she wailed. "What if I'm wrong? What if she's telling the truth?"

Michael sighed. "Why don't we wait a day or two? Maybe she'll tell us what's going on."

"You think she will?" Logan asked his brother.

"I hope so."

Dani parked her car under a tree near the entrance to the ranch driveway. She didn't hear the sound of the nightly dinner bell, but she watched as Floyd came out of the barn and went into the house. With a sigh she saw Michael leave the manager's house and head in for dinner, too.

That was what she was waiting for.

She started her car and slowly drove down the drive, trying to be as quiet as possible. Tonight she wasn't here to enjoy the friendly conversation and good-natured laughter around the Circle K table. No, she had another purpose tonight: get her stuff, without being seen.

Dani maintained a stoic expression as she methodically packed her clothes in the two bags she'd brought with her. After stowing them in the trunk of her car, she added the kitchen things she'd purchased on her shopping trip with Abby and Ellen. That thought almost broke her. She'd felt such joy only yesterday.

The urge to cry had her speeding up her movements. She had to get out of there before she fell to her knees and begged them to take her back, reassuring them she didn't want their money. She wanted their love. But she couldn't stay. Abby no longer trusted her.

She filled a paper sack with her groceries, including the five yogurts in the refrigerator. Then she left the house she'd already called home after only two nights and drove away, quietly.

They were halfway through their roast beef dinner when the phone rang. It had been a quiet meal. Even Mirabelle and Scotty must have sensed the sadness at the table; they sat like little angels.

Logan got up and went to the phone. "Hello?"

"Hey, Logan, it's Jed."

"Hi, Jed, what's up?" He hadn't talked to Beth's husband in several days.

"I'm not sure anything is, but…I just thought I'd mention it. Dani drives a blue Chevy, doesn't she?"

Logan's hand tightened on the receiver. "Yeah, that's Dani's car. Why?" By the time he finished with that question, Michael and Abby were beside him.

"Well, I saw her car parked under the tree by our driveway. Then she drove slowly in to the manager's house, loaded a few things and drove out. She was heading for town."

"Thanks for the info, Jed."

"No problem. If you need help, let me know."

"I will."

After hanging up the phone, he told his wife and brother what Jed had said. Without a word, Michael immediately went out the back door.

He rushed into his house and opened Dani's bedroom door. The closet was open. And empty. Her bed was still made, but then Abby had loaned her the sheets and bed cover. Even the new pillows she'd bought were missing.

"Damn!" he exclaimed, his hands on his hips. He didn't realize Abby had followed him until he heard her voice from behind him.

"I'm sorry, Michael. I guess you were right. I shouldn't have trusted her."

"I think you're wrong, Abby," Michael said slowly as he turned around.

"What? You were the one convinced she was running a scam."

Logan, who had come in behind Abby, said, "She's right, Michael. You were the one who warned Abby not to be taken in."

"Did she ask for her check back?" Michael asked.

"No. But she could stop payment on it," Logan pointed out.

"I'll bet she doesn't."

"Then why did she run away?" Abby asked.

"My guess is she realized you doubted her. She never attempted to move in. You insisted. She offered to pay because she wouldn't take anything free. That was a lesson she apparently learned at an early age."

"Now you believe her?" Abby shrieked. "After warning me?"

Michael lowered his head. "I know, Abby. But she's impressive in the office. She's no dummy."

"I never thought she was." Abby's voice was strong, sure, and she faced Michael squarely.

The three of them stood there staring at each other.

"So what do we do now?" Logan finally asked.

"I think you should go ahead and talk to those friends of Beulah," Michael said to Abby. "It would be nice to know if Dani really is kin to Beulah."

"You're right, it would. And I don't need her to do that," Abby said, thinking aloud.

Michael ran a hand through his hair. "I'll wait until tomorrow at work and see if I can get her to talk."

"You think she'll turn up at work tomorrow?" Logan asked.

"Yeah. It'll look bad on her résumé to be at a job for a couple of weeks."

Logan looked at his brother. "But would she care? Are you sure she really has a law degree? That she really passed the bar?"

Michael wanted to defend Dani, but he reminded himself that he should be cautious. Just because he wanted her to be honest didn't mean she was. Like the lawyer he was, he had to get the facts. "I'll check those things out."

"And if we find out she's honest, will she ever speak to us again?" Abby whispered, tears suddenly welling in her eyes.

Michael put his arm around her. "I don't know, Abby. But I hope so."

In fact, he had just discovered how much he'd looked forward to getting to know Dani better.

He was eager for tomorrow.

Dani told herself her place of residence made no difference. She would be fine in the walk-up apartment in a low-rent area. At least here she could rent by the week until she decided what to do. She swiftly dismissed the joy she'd felt, living with the Kennedy clan. Though the furnishings were spartan, her personal items around the apartment made it feel more like hers. Nevertheless, she felt out of sorts, anxious, and slept little all night.

In the morning she got to work early, wanting to settle in before Michael arrived. He might not even bring up her absence, she told herself. But she wanted to be prepared, just in case.

When she entered her office, long before the secretary had taken her post outside her door, Dani discovered she wasn't as prepared as she'd hoped.

Michael was sitting in the guest chair in front of her desk.

"Why don't you close the door, Dani? I think you want our chat to be private."

She drew a deep breath, hoping it was the only indication of her distress. She didn't need to show weakness now. Closing the door, she turned and walked to her desk. She was glad she'd worn her most professional suit. She was going to need all the confidence she could muster.

"Good morning, Michael." She sat down behind her desk and folded her hands together in front of her. If she kept them tightly together, she reasoned, he wouldn't notice they were shaking.

"Did you have a good night, Dani?"

"Yes, thank you."

"Where did you spend it?" he asked in a casual tone of voice that didn't match the spark she saw in his dark eyes.

"In my own bed," she said, staring at her hands.

"Funny. I thought your bed was in my house. I thought you paid a month's rent. Do you want your money back?"

"No." She stopped there, because she needed that money back. She didn't have a lot to spare, but she wasn't going to ask for it.

"What happened? Did you decide you didn't like the neighborhood?"

She looked up at him, hurt but doing her best to hide it. "We both know what happened. Abby realized she'd made a mistake and regretted her generosity. I didn't want to take advantage of her, so I left." There, she'd clearly stated the situation. Now she prayed he'd leave her alone. She didn't know how long she could hold back the tears.

"Abby didn't want you to leave." The gentleness in his voice was almost her undoing.

"Yes, she did, Michael. She may not yet be able to see that clearly, but I could. Why cause her more stress just because she was generous? I'll write her a note apologizing for leaving without saying goodbye."

"And that's how you want to leave it?" he asked, studying her.

"Yes." Her heart was beginning to ache. At least she thought that was what was happening. "Please go away now. I have some work I need to do."

To her relief, Michael stood. His tall, lean and muscled body looked invincible to her and left a longing in her soul she didn't want to identify.

"Okay, I'll go. But this is not the end of things. Abby deserves more than that."

Michael went to his office. He'd hurt Dani with his last remark. He'd seen it in her eyes. He felt bad about his behavior, but she wore armor that made it difficult to get through to her.

He made phone calls to Amarillo and Lubbock, checking up on her, until it was time to appear in court. He hurried out to the lobby where Dick and Dani were waiting.

"Sorry, time got away from me. Did I keep you waiting?" he asked Dick.

"Nope. We're right on time. It's not far to the courthouse. We'll all go in my car."

Michael said nothing, but Dick's decision made his plans a little more difficult. He intended to kidnap Dani for lunch.

Thanks to the solid evidence and their well-prepared witness who performed well under pressure, the morning went well.

By the time the judge called a two-hour lunch break, Dick was ecstatic. "Ned is going to be really pleased with the way things went. Dani, it was your work with the witness that made her so strong. Good job."

"Thank you, Dick," Dani returned professionally.

"How about I treat us to lunch today? You both deserve it," Dick said, a smile still lighting up his face.

"Thanks, Dick, but I'm taking Dani to lunch. We need to talk about…things."

The word was out before she could stop it or monitor her tone. "No! No, it—"

"It's okay, honey," Michael said, putting his arm around her and dropping a brief kiss on her lips. "Ned told Dick about us. It's no surprise to him." Then he swept Dani out of the courtroom.

"Take your hands off me," she snapped as they reached the hallway.

"Come on, Dani, I'm not pawing you. I'm just being friendly. There's a café just across the street we can go to." He pulled back his arm in an exaggerated manner. "And don't worry. You'll be safe."

Once they were seated in a booth in the back and had placed their orders, she folded her hands on the table and calmly said, "Well?"

"Well what?" he asked, taking a sip of his cola the waitress had delivered.

"Why did we have to have lunch together?"

"To preserve the rumors of our office romance that keeps you out of Ned's scope."

"There's no need to pretend anymore." Her voice was stiff, but she couldn't continue to act as if everything was all right.

"I think there is. Even if you lied about Beulah, it doesn't mean you should be treated the way Ned was treating you."

She closed her eyes, wanting to hide the devastation his words wreaked on her. So he, too, thought she'd lied. A long time ago she'd learned that honesty was the most precious commodity. Too bad Michael didn't know that about her.

"I see," was all she said.

The waitress returned with their orders, cutting off their conversation. Michael enjoyed the delicious aroma wafting up from the meat loaf. Then he eyed the meager salad in front of Dani, some tired lettuce leaves in a small bowl, with a packet of salad dressing.

"You can go ahead and bring her dinner now," he told the waitress.

The older woman gave him a bewildered look.

"This is all I ordered, Michael," Dani interjected. "Thank you," she told to the waitress.

"Are you on a diet?"

She ignored him.

"Logan isn't going to cash your check, Dani, if you're worried about money."

"There's no reason why he shouldn't. It's not his fault that I changed my mind. It's legally his right to cash it."

"Where are you living now?" he asked abruptly.

"It doesn't matter. I've found a place. I'm not sleeping on the streets, or wherever else you're imagining, Michael. I'm not Cinderella waiting to be rescued."

Switching topics, Michael brought up his morning's work. "I checked on your law school career. It's valid. I called Austin to make sure you'd passed the bar."

"You could've gotten that information from Ned," she reminded him, daintily eating her salad.

"It would've looked strange if I'd asked him for details of my girlfriend's past, don't you think?"

She merely shrugged.

"Dani, I'm trying to help you."

She carefully laid down her fork and looked at him. "I'm glad you verified my education, if you needed that assurance to work with me. That's all I want with you, a working relationship. I don't need any other help from you, Michael." Her gaze remained steady on him. "I'm not going to live on the Kennedy ranch. I'm not going to be best friends with Abby or Ellen or anyone else I met Saturday. We have nothing to discuss." She opened her purse and put out a few dollars on the table. "That's for my lunch. I'll see you in the courtroom at two o'clock."

She walked out of the café, leaving a stunned Michael wondering what he should say or do.

Abby and Ellen entered the nursing home at lunchtime, having left a cooked meal on the kitchen table. Floyd was going to stay in for the afternoon and watch over the kids.

"Hello, Mrs. Gardner," Abby said to the woman who ran the nursing home. "Ellen and I thought we'd visit with Molly Barnes and Betty Collins today, since we were out."

"Well, of course they'll be delighted to have visitors." The middle-aged director came around her desk and ushered them in. "Come along. I'll show you to their table."

She led them to a large room with a number of tables and a sea of white-headed ladies and a few gentlemen. "There they are, at the table by the window."

Abby thanked Mrs. Gardner for her assistance, then

she and Ellen made their way among the tables till they reached the two elderly ladies. After reintroductions, Abby got right to the point. "Do you remember Beulah Kennedy, my great-aunt?"

The smaller of the two ladies spoke up. "Why, 'course I do," Molly replied, adjusting her glasses, which hung on a beaded chain. "We was best friends all our lives. Where is she?" The old lady began looking around, as if she expected Beulah to appear.

"I'm afraid she's dead, Molly," Abby said, feeling sorry for the woman's confusion. "That's why I've come to see you."

"I went to her funeral," Betty interjected. "Sad. That was really sad," she muttered, looking away.

"Yes, it was," Ellen concurred. "Beulah was such a good woman."

All the ladies agreed.

"Do you remember if Beulah ever had a child?" Abby held her breath as she waited for an answer.

"No," Betty said. "She and her husband never had a baby. She wanted one, though."

"I'm sure she did. She would've made a great mother," Abby was disappointed that her fears had been confirmed.

"You'd think so," Molly said, "but when her daughter came to see her, she didn't want nothing to do with her."

Abby and Ellen looked at each other. Then Abby said quietly, "Her daughter? She had a daughter?"

"Not really," Molly replied, appearing to have difficulty scooping up her English peas.

"I don't understand, Molly," Abby said, gently

taking the spoon from Molly's hand. "Let me help you with the peas." After putting the vegetables in Molly's mouth, she tried again. "Was it her daughter who came to see her?"

"Said she was. But Beulah didn't like her."

"Then she had a daughter?"

When Molly nodded, Betty looked alarmed. "You promised you wouldn't tell!"

Ellen patted Betty's shoulder. "It's important that we know, Betty. Beulah wouldn't mind."

"Well then, okay." Betty nodded. "Beulah had herself a daughter. Sure did."

Chapter Seven

Betty and Molly told them about Beulah's unwed pregnancy. They also recounted the time that a young woman had come to find Beulah, claiming to be that child. But Beulah told them the girl had been greedy, only after what she could get.

Abby was reminded of her arrival, with her sisters, at the Circle K ranch. It was nothing more than two small houses in shabby condition, and a few sheds and one barn, all in need of care. Abby and her sisters had thought their aunt was destitute, but Beulah had given them a chance to be together, and they were grateful.

It was only upon her death that they'd discovered all their hard work had been unnecessary. Beulah had left them millions of dollars she'd saved from the four oil wells that had once pumped oil twenty-four hours a day. The wells had dried up by the time they'd arrived, but Beulah had wisely invested the money.

The three of them had been stunned, Abby remembered clearly. Afterward, they invested money in refurbishing the ranch, making it the comfortable home it was now.

She smiled as she saw the white two-story house with a broad porch as they turned into the driveway at the ranch.

Ellen went off to fix them a pot of hot tea. Aunt Beulah had loved her tea, she told Abby.

When they sat down with their steaming cups. Ellen said, "So, we know that Dani's story could be true."

"Yes. I feel terrible for doubting her now."

"I don't think you should. We don't know for sure that the woman who came was really Beulah's child."

"And I don't know how to prove it."

"I have a friend who worked in social services for years," Ellen said. "She probably wasn't working there when Beulah gave away her baby, but she might know who to call to find out. We might find out her adopted name."

"I doubt that she used her adopted name. She sounds like a scam artist of the worst kind if she came to Beulah's only wanting money."

"I bet she left thinking Beulah was the poorest lady in the county," Ellen said with a chuckle.

"Call your friend and see what you can find out," Abby requested. "I'll go upstairs and relieve Floyd. I suddenly feel the need to hug my children."

Michael waited in his office for Dani to leave. When she finally walked down the hall with her briefcase, he was right behind her.

She must have heard his footsteps behind her and looked over her shoulder. "Good night, Michael."

"Good night, Dani. Got plans for tonight?"

"Yes, I do."

Jealousy surged through him. She'd already found someone else to provide her entertainment?

"Who is he?"

She stopped and turned to stare at him. "I beg your pardon?"

"I mean…I just wondered if you'd made friends with anyone else."

Ned stepped out of his office, his eyes wide with what he'd just heard. "Is there discord between the two of you?"

"No, not at all," Michael said, moving forward to put his arm around Dani. "She worries about appearances. I told her it doesn't matter, that everyone will know soon. We all know how the gossip flies."

"Hmm, yes, I suppose you're right." Ned turned to walk down the hall. "Good night, you two."

Neither of them moved until he had left the building.

"That was close," Michael said on a sigh.

"I told you it wasn't necessary to continue the charade. I'm not your responsibility." Dani pulled away and started down the hall.

"Are you going to make me follow you?" he asked, his voice hard.

She stopped and turned. "Why would you?"

Michael couldn't quite believe the innocence he saw in her eyes.

"Maybe because I'm worried about you. I want to be sure you're safe."

She actually laughed. "Michael, I'm twenty-five years old, an adult. If I'm not safe, it's my fault. It's got nothing to do with you." She spun on her heel and continued on her way.

He tightened his lips and started after her. Maybe she wasn't his business, but he thought she was. Before he went home today he intended to know where she was living.

He followed her to a local grocery store, where he waited in his car for her to emerge with a small bag. If that was her grocery shopping, either she wasn't a big eater or she was short of money. He wanted to buy more groceries and take them to her, but he knew he'd be ignored.

She was an independent woman.

He remembered Lindsay's complaints when she was younger. His sister had claimed she couldn't take a breath of air without one of her brothers wanting to make sure she didn't choke. Her father, too, had wanted his daughter to be safe, no matter how smothered she felt.

Michael didn't think Dani had ever been smothered by someone caring too much. He was sure her independence came from no one caring enough.

It was difficult to go home once he saw where she was living. The apartment house had seen better days, in a low-income neighborhood. While Dani carried her grocery sack upstairs, he went to the office and asked about the rental terms. The manager had been suspicious about his request, with good reason. They were weekly rentals.

Michael went back to his car and spent almost half an hour convincing himself that Dani would be okay. He wanted to go in there and sweep her into his arms and carry her away. But unlike Cinderella, Dani wouldn't appreciate his high-handedness.

On the drive back to the Circle K, he tried to think of options that would get Dani back to the ranch. But there weren't any. If she didn't want to be friends with any of them, he couldn't force her.

Frustrated, he parked by Logan and Abby's house. It was dinnertime, and his lunch hadn't stayed with him, which only reminded him of the salad Dani had eaten, and fueled his frustration.

As he entered, he said, "Logan, you can't cash that check."

Already enjoying his dinner, Logan finished chewing the bite he'd just taken before he said, "I have no intention of cashing the check."

"Good."

"What is it, Michael? Why are you upset?" Abby looked a little upset herself.

"She's living in a rundown apartment house that rents by the week. She bought a few groceries, but no more than half a bag. And for lunch she had a salad that was enough to maybe feed a bird, and then insisted on paying for it." He looked at the full plates on the table and didn't think he could eat.

"Didn't you tell her we wouldn't cash the check?" Abby asked.

"Yeah. She said Logan had a legal right to cash it."

"What's wrong, Uncle Mike?" Mirabelle asked, staring at him.

Michael looked at the child's innocent face, which reminded him of the questions he had about Dani's childhood. Had anyone ever been there for her? Had she even gotten the hugs and kisses that were an everyday event for Mirabelle?

"Nothing's wrong, honey," he told her in a gentle voice. "I'm just worried about Dani."

"Why?" the little girl asked.

"Because I don't think she had a good mommy like you have."

"Why not?"

"Mirabelle," Abby said quietly, "no more questions. Eat your dinner. I think Ellen made banana pudding for dessert tonight."

"Oh, yummy," the child exclaimed, her attention drawn away from Michael.

"Is she doing all right?" Abby asked, staring at Michael.

He shrugged his shoulders. "I don't think she's in a safe place, but I can't figure how to change things. I have no right to protect her."

Logan looked at his daughter and then at Michael. "Yeah. I understand. And I understand Dad a lot better than I ever have before."

Michael nodded.

Abby cleared her throat. "I went to the nursing home today."

She paused and Michael showed his impatience. "And?" he prompted.

Abby swallowed. "Beulah did have a baby before she married our uncle. She gave it up for adoption."

As silence descended upon the room, Ellen spoke up. "How about I fix bowls of pudding for you and the children, Floyd, and you go find a program on television for all of you?"

Floyd read between the lines and quickly agreed. The children were happy to abandon their vegetables. After situating them, Ellen returned to the table. "I heard from my friend. She's going to call tomorrow."

Michael frowned. "Your friend?"

"I have a friend who used to work with the social services people. She thought she might be able to find out something."

Abby snapped her fingers. "I should have called Melissa, too. She works with them regarding the foster children. Maybe she can find out something."

"That's a good idea," Logan said. He turned to his brother. "You can assure Dani I won't be cashing her check."

"I know," Michael said wearily. "I don't think she'll believe me, though."

Abby leaned forward and touched his arm. "Michael, I'm so sorry," she said, lowering her voice. "This is all my fault. Everything was fine until I tried to prove Dani's story. That's what made her think I didn't believe her. But I was trying to do the right thing. If she's Beulah's granddaughter, she *should* have a share of Beulah's estate."

"Legally you're wrong. She couldn't get a penny."

"Come on, Michael, that can't be right," Logan protested. "If she's her granddaughter, of course she'd be entitled to something."

"If Beulah knew about her existence, or her mother's existence, when she wrote her will, then no, Dani doesn't have a right to Beulah's estate. Beulah, knowing of her daughter's existence, chose to leave everything to Abby and her sisters. She had that right."

"I don't care," Abby protested. "I won't stand for Beulah's granddaughter living in poverty while we live like we do!"

Logan tried to calm her down. "Well, we don't know if she really is kin, honey, so don't get upset."

"But I'm mad at myself. She's a wonderful person and I ruined everything."

"Maybe we both did, Abby," Michael said softly.

Worried about Dani's safety, Michael didn't get much sleep that night. There had been some derelicts hanging around the apartment house last night. What if they attacked her this morning? Whom would she call for help?

Not him.

He was up before dawn, thanks to a nightmare in which Dani played a starring role. Giving up on getting back to sleep he took his shower and dressed in his work clothes. Then, instead of heading to Logan's house for breakfast, he got in his car and drove into Wichita Falls.

After driving through a fast-food place and getting

some breakfast, he drove to Dani's apartment house and parked where he could see her front door.

About an hour later, a little after seven, he saw Dani emerge from her apartment with two suitcases in hand. After putting those in her car, she went back up the stairs. She came back down with a sack full of something and put it in the car. Then she got behind the wheel and backed out.

Was she changing residences or leaving town? He had no idea, but his heart was thumping as he followed her. The thought of losing all contact with Dani Langston bothered him.

She turned in at a middle-class apartment house, in reasonable repair, with a lot of cars in the parking spaces. She parked in front of the third unit and got out to unlock the first door she came to.

Obviously, she'd made arrangements last night. Good. At least he wouldn't lose sleep wondering about her being attacked. He hoped, anyway. He waited for half an hour before she finally came out and got in her car, driving in the direction of the office. When she reached it, he parked beside her and stood on the pavement. "Good morning," he called as soon as she opened her door.

She appeared startled, but calmly greeted him. "Good morning, Michael."

She reached for her briefcase and then walked past him as he stood waiting.

Catching up, he fell into stride with her. "We should be out of court before noon today."

"I hope so."

"Do you have anything to work on afterward?"

"No, but I'm hoping Ned will assign me to a case with Dick's recommendation."

"Probably. You did nice work for him."

"Thank you."

"Is work all we're going to talk about?" He knew he was being impatient, but he couldn't help himself.

"Yes," she said succinctly, and opened the door to the building.

"How about dinner this evening? I'd like to take you out."

"Why?" She didn't misstep or hesitate as she walked down the hall.

"Because you're a beautiful, intelligent woman."

"No, thank you. I don't believe in mixing work with pleasure."

Since that was his own opinion, too, he couldn't think of anything to say. Dani went into her office and closed her door.

Michael's office was across the hall, with the secretary's desk in between them. If he stared at Dani's door, the woman manning the desk would think he was staring at her. He kept his door open, hoping to stay busy.

He'd almost forgotten to call the ranch and explain why he didn't show up for breakfast. He was feeling ungrateful, even as he resented having to report in. After years on his own, he was used to his independence.

Ellen answered the phone, and he explained, "I went in early this morning. That's why I didn't show up for breakfast. I hope that's okay."

"Of course it is," Ellen said easily. "I'll tell Abby

when she comes in for lunch. She worries, you know.''

''Yeah. Give her my apology, please.''

''Sure thing.''

Michael spent the rest of his morning in court until about eleven-thirty. The prosecution had rested their case the day before, but the defense had a right to its rebuttal. When the lawyer representing the businessman who had propositioned the young woman they represented announced his case was complete, the judge instructed the jury and told them to return to the courtroom at two o'clock so they could begin determining the man's fate.

Dick began packing his briefcase. ''I feel good about this one, boys and girls,'' he announced with a smile. ''I bet we get a verdict this afternoon.''

''That soon?'' Michael asked.

''I agree,'' Dani said. ''The defendant looked so hangdog at the end, I thought he was going to confess right there.''

''I think he's tougher than that,'' Michael said. ''I think he's playing the jury for sympathy.''

Dani sighed. ''You're probably right,'' she admitted. ''I tend to be too optimistic.''

As she started out of the courtroom, Michael touched her arm. ''Lunch?''

''No, thank you.'' She kept walking. Since they'd both ridden over with Dick, Michael didn't know where she was going. He asked Dick if Dani had said anything about riding back with him, and he said no.

When they got to Dick's car, there was no sign of her. They waited for about five minutes. Then Dick suggested they go to the office. "She might have gotten a ride from a friend."

Michael didn't tell him that Dani had no friends in Wichita Falls. He kept his eyes peeled on the short drive back to the office.

His vigilance paid off when he saw her walking briskly along.

At his request Dick pulled over and Michael got out. After thanking Dick for the ride, he promised he'd be back at the office shortly. Then he turned in the direction to intersect Dani's path. "Why didn't you ride with us?" he asked when he was in front of her.

Dani stopped and stared at him. "I thought a brisk walk would be good for me."

"I wish you'd said something. I could've joined you."

"I wanted to think about some things. I'm afraid I wasn't prepared to entertain."

"I see. What about lunch?"

"No, thank you."

"You have to eat, Dani. I've found a good restaurant not far away. Let me treat you to lunch for once."

"There's no reason for you to treat me to lunch, Michael. We work together. And that's all." She walked around him and continued toward the office.

"What if I want more?"

It took several days before Abby had gathered enough information to be sure that Dani was indeed Beulah's granddaughter as she'd suggested when she first arrived. Her birth mother's name was the same as that of the adopting couple.

Abby had found records of Dani's birth. Just as Dani had said, her mother was forty when Dani was born. Abby couldn't help thinking about a small child like Mirabelle being neglected or mistreated by a woman who didn't want her.

Before she told Michael about what she'd found out, she invited her two sisters over for tea. Ellen offered to serve it in Abby's office, so she could be alone with her sisters, but Abby refused.

"I want you to be here, Ellen. You're part of the family."

Ellen smiled, and the wrinkles around her mouth and eyes emphasized her innate gentleness and wisdom. She went off to bake special tea cakes for the meeting.

Beth was the first to arrive. "Wow! I love these little cakes, Ellen. What's the occasion?"

Ellen turned a bright red. "I just felt like making them. You know Floyd loves them, too."

Beth looked puzzled. "So Floyd's joining us, too?"

"No! No, I baked extra for him."

Before Beth could ask anything else, Ellen hurried down the hall to Abby's office. "Oh, Abby, I didn't mean to give anything away, but Beth saw the tea cakes and wanted to know what's the occasion. I'm so sorry."

"Ellen, calm down. It's okay. I'm going to tell them at once. But you should've known," Abby added, hoping to relieve Ellen's alarm with a little teasing. "Beth always had a sweet tooth."

"I know. I should've thought—"

"Ellen," Abby said, stopping her. "I was teasing. None of us could resist your baking. Quit worrying." They went into the kitchen arm in arm.

Melissa had arrived, and she and Beth were whispering at the table.

Beth jumped to her feet. "I knew it!" She ran to put her arms around Ellen. "Something's wrong, isn't it? Are you sick? Is it Floyd? Oh, dear, what can we do?"

Abby pulled her sister back to the table. "Sit down, Chicken Little. The sky isn't falling in right now."

Melissa, sitting quietly at the table, looked at Abby. "But there is something wrong?"

"Not wrong, exactly," Abby said, "but I'm concerned about something."

Ellen put a flowered teapot on the table and the plate of tea cakes. She'd carefully set the table as Aunt Beulah used to do.

"Come on, Ellen. Let's sit down. Everything's perfect," Abby assured the housekeeper. "We're having tea like Aunt Beulah used to like on Sunday afternoons, because we need to discuss her."

"Why?" Beth demanded.

Melissa waited silently.

"Do you remember Dani?" Abby asked.

Both of her sisters frowned, obviously thinking of the implications of her question.

Melissa answered first. "Yes, we do, of course. Why?"

Ellen passed the plate of tea cakes, but even Beth rejected them.

Abby sighed. ''I suggested to Dani that we go to the nursing home together and ask several of Beulah's friends if Beulah had ever had a child.''

''That's a good idea,'' Beth said at once.

Abby exchanged glances with Ellen, then said, ''Well, it upset her. She thought I didn't trust her and she moved out of the manager's house into town.''

''Then she must've been lying,'' Beth deduced. ''Otherwise why would it bother her?''

Melissa turned to her sister. ''Wouldn't it bother you if Abby didn't trust you, Beth?''

''Well, yes, but Abby's my sister. Dani just came out of the blue and expected us to believe her. That's asking for too much.''

''Maybe.'' Abby took a sip of tea. ''Michael and I discussed the problem, and he suggested I check into Dani's story. He said legally Dani has no right to Beulah's estate. But I might feel better if I discovered whether Dani was telling the truth.''

Melissa frowned. ''Did she ever ask for anything? Did she ask to live here?''

Abby put down he tea cup and shook her head. ''No, that was my idea. She insisted on paying rent.''

''So she still lives here?'' Melissa asked.

''No. She left that night. Jed called and told us he'd seen her drive in, pack up and drive out.''

Melissa paused as she reached out for a tea cake and looked up at her sister. ''Without telling you?''

''Yes, without telling us.''

''Have you talked to her?''

"She's not taking my calls at the office, and I don't have a number for her other than that."

"So what is it we need to discuss?" Melissa asked.

"The fact that she *is* Beulah's granddaughter. I've proven it."

Chapter Eight

Dani's new apartment was an improvement on her first. It was reasonably clean and in working order. Even better, the other renters didn't scare her.

That thought brought to mind her would-be protector. Michael tempted her so much, but his connection to Abby made any relationship impossible. Besides, she worked with him, though Ned had now assigned them to different cases after they won the harassment case.

Michael was the lead attorney on his cases, while she was a worker bee on the two she'd been assigned. The cases involved women, too, of course. But at least she was doing legal work. Finally everything was settling into place. As she sat back at her desk, she felt a smile tug at her lips. Tonight she was treating herself with a long hot bubble bath and new novel.

"Ms. Langston?"

Dani looked up to see the secretary at her door. "Yes, Angie?"

"You just received another call from Mrs. Crawford. Am I still supposed to tell her you're not available?"

"No. I'll give her a call. Do you have her number?"

The woman handed her a message form with Abby's number. Under the number was the message, requesting she call right away.

She drew a deep breath and dialed the number. When Abby answered, she began. "It's Dani. I need to apologize for leaving like I did." She'd intended to write a note, but finding a decent place to live had taken top priority.

"Thanks for saying that, Dani, but the fault was mine. My sisters and I want to talk to you. Can we meet for lunch?"

Dani could tell something was up, but she had no idea why Beth and Melissa would come. "Why?"

Abby ignored that question. "Is today all right?"

"Today?" What was so urgent? Dani thought. "I...I guess so."

"Good. Shall we meet at Sunny's? It's just a block from your office."

"Yes, I've been there."

"All right. We'll see you at eleven forty-five."

Dani hung up the phone, but she continued to stare at it. She wanted to know what was going on before she met them for lunch.

Michael. He would know.

The door to his office was closed, she could see.

She walked out to the secretary's desk. "Does Mr. Crawford have someone with him?"

"No. He said he needed to concentrate."

"Oh. Well, I have something I need to discuss with him. Could you call him and see if it's okay if I come in?"

Though she gave Dani a strange look, Angie called Michael on the intercom. "He says to come in."

"Thank you."

When she opened the door, Michael was standing at his desk, waiting for her.

"What's wrong, Dani?"

"What makes you think something is wrong?" She could barely look at him, hating to lie.

"Because you chose to come to my office. You've been avoiding me."

"I've been busy."

He sat back in his desk chair, assuming a relaxed pose. "So how are your cases going?"

"Fine. Yours?"

"Fine." He shot her a sly smile, as if he saw right through her. "Enough of the niceties, Dani. What's wrong?"

She slipped her hands in her skirt pockets and started pacing. "Abby called. When I called her back, I apologized for leaving as I did. She said okay, but she and her sisters want to have lunch with me today."

"That's nice," Michael said in a noncommittal voice, and he looked away from her.

"So what's up?"

"What do you mean?" he asked.

"You're not the only one who knows when someone is hiding something. You know the reason for the invitation. What is it?"

He lifted his gaze to her face. "Don't you think Abby could have answered that question?"

"She could've, but she seemed in a hurry. Look, Michael, I'm going to meet them, but I like to be prepared for what's coming. I thought you might give me a heads-up."

He came around his desk and took her by the shoulders. "Dani, Abby wouldn't hurt you, no matter what. Go to lunch and everything will be all right," he insisted. Then, as if he couldn't resist, he pulled her into his arms and covered her lips.

Dani didn't intend to respond. The brief kisses Michael had given her had been intriguing, tempting, but she promised herself to stay uninvolved. Once his warm mouth touched hers, her intentions flew out the window. His strong arms wrapped around her and she felt a combination of safety and love—two emotions that were rare in her life.

She pulled away from the hunger of his lips. "W-we shouldn't be doing this," she whispered hoarsely.

"Yes, we should," he muttered, his gaze fixed on her lips. Then he took them again, this time with more insistence, drawing her into a deeper connection.

Dani could think of nothing, process nothing but the feel of his mouth and tongue. She could stay in his arms forever. But forever wasn't meant to be, as they were interrupted by a booming voice.

"Michael, can you—" It was Ned stepping into Michael's office.

Dani tried to escape Michael's arms, but he held on to her. He did stop kissing her, however. She said nothing, could think of nothing to say.

Ned stood there, similarly frozen.

Finally Michael asked, "What do you need, Ned? Is there something you want me to do?"

"I received a call from a friend about one of the cases I gave you. I need to discuss it with you—when you have time." Sarcasm crept into his voice.

"I'll be in your office in five minutes," Michael said calmly. "Which case is it?"

"The Blackburn case," Ned said as he turned and left the room.

"Are you okay?" Michael asked, kissing her forehead.

That gentle touch was almost more than she could bear. She pulled away, and this time he let her go. "We shouldn't be doing that." Her voice was thin and she barely recognized it.

"Why?"

His question took her by surprise. "We work together. I thought we'd decided—"

"Well, technically that's true."

"Technically? What do you mean?"

He touched her again, drawing a finger down her soft cheek. "I met you before we started working together, Dani. That makes a difference."

She stepped back. "No, it doesn't!"

Michael opened his mouth to speak, but stopped, as if he rethought his words. "Go to lunch, Dani. I'll talk to you afterward." He escorted her to the door and opened it. With Angie watching them, he dropped a brief kiss on her lips. "See you after lunch."

Dani's cheeks were bright red as she hurried back to her office and closed the door. What was she going to do? A few minutes ago she'd thought everything was settling down. She was beginning to think she could stay at the D.A.'s office for a year and then find another job without the change hurting her.

It had been a good plan.

Except she hadn't factored in Michael. With a brilliant career in front of him, the man wasn't going anywhere. And he wanted her.

The worst discovery of the morning was her weakness for him. Now she realized she was fighting herself as much as him.

The reality hit her: she would have to leave at once, no matter what it did to her career.

"There she is." Abby stood and waved at Dani who entered the restaurant.

"She looks alarmed," Melissa said softly.

"Why would she be worried?" Beth asked. "Are we sure she's not just after the money?"

"It doesn't matter, Beth. We've made our decision. We're doing this for Beulah, for all she gave us," Melissa reminded her sister.

Abby had walked forward to greet Dani. "Thank you for coming."

Dani took Abby's hand and nodded, but she didn't speak. She was afraid her control wasn't strong enough. When they reached the table, she nodded at Beth and Melissa, too.

"Shall we order first?" Abby asked, looking at Dani. "I can recommend the chicken Alfredo. It's my favorite."

"Then I'll take that," Dani said, not caring what she ordered. She figured she wouldn't be there long enough to eat much of it.

Once the waitress left the table, Dani looked at Abby, knowing she would be the one to tell her why they were all having lunch together.

Abby ducked her head, then she looked up. "I apologize for upsetting you when I suggested we go to the nursing home. But why did it, Dani?"

"It doesn't matter," she said, her voice showing no emotion as she stared at her folded hands on the table.

"Yes, it does. But I went to the nursing home, anyway, with Ellen."

Dani said nothing.

"I found out that Beulah had a baby before she married our uncle, and she gave her up for adoption."

Dani nodded. She'd already known that.

"The child was adopted by a couple named Langston." Abby paused again, to see if Dani wanted to say anything.

When she didn't, Beth, more impatient, leaned forward. "Doesn't that surprise you?"

"No. I knew all this." Dani still showed no emotion.

"Do you know that your mother came to see Beulah?" Beth continued.

"Yes."

"If you knew all this information, why didn't you just tell us Beulah was your grandmother?"

Dani shook her head but said nothing.

"Dani," Abby said insistently, "we want you to be part of our family. You *are* family."

"Not really. There's no blood relationship," Dani said stoically.

Melissa smiled. "Beulah could have said that when we were orphaned. They were going to separate us, you know." She swallowed. "We were clinging to each other, so afraid, then Beulah stepped in and claimed us. She said we were her great-nieces and she took us home with her."

Abby spoke next. "Beulah became our mother, or grandmother, as she was to you. We received the wisdom, care and love that you should've had. Maybe you've had a good life, but whether you did or not, we owe you."

Dani didn't take a breath before she set Abby straight. "No! No, you don't owe me. All I wanted when I came to the ranch was to make sure Beulah was okay if she was alive... And I wanted to know if—I wanted to find something good about someone kin to me." She bowed her head, fighting her control. When she looked up, she smiled through the tears escaping her eyes. "You gave me that. I learned that my grandmother was a respected woman and a loving one. That was a precious gift."

Abby reached out and clasped her hand. "I'm so glad we could do that for you. But we had in mind something more substantial. We aren't offering part of the ranch because that gets too complicated, but we've arranged for a fourth of the money to be put in your name. You can withdraw it and deposit it into another account, with another financial advisor, but we recommend Joe Bell. He's been very good with ours.''

Dani stared at Abby, trying to understand what she was saying. When it finally pierced her brain, she jumped up from the table. ''No! I don't want it. Beulah wouldn't want me to have it. I…I have to go!''

She ran out of the restaurant.

Michael closed his door and ate the sandwich he'd bought at the minimart on the corner. He was worried about what was happening at the restaurant with the ladies.

He wasn't sure what Dani's reaction would be to their generosity. It was strange how well he felt he knew Dani. But as much as he'd tried to tell himself he was only guessing, he didn't think she'd accept the money.

When a knock sounded at his door, he leaped to his feet and rushed to open it. The three women at his door told him he'd been right.

''What happened?'' he demanded.

''Can we come in?'' Abby asked.

''Oh, sure. Sorry.'' He held the door open and backed up to give them room.

After Abby, Beth and Melissa sat down, Michael rounded his desk and sat down, too. ''Now, what happened? You didn't have time to eat much.''

''We didn't eat anything,'' Beth complained.

Michael said nothing, but his heart was beating double time.

Abby leaned forward. "We explained that we knew she was Beulah's granddaughter. She already knew that, Michael. She didn't need the proof."

Michael nodded. "I'm not really surprised."

"Anyway, I explained that we weren't going to cut up the ranch, but we were willing to share the money with her. She acted as if I was talking gibberish. Then, as if it finally made sense, she jumped to her feet, rejected our offer and ran out."

Michael sat with his head down and said nothing.

"Did she come back here?" Melissa asked.

"I'll check." Michael picked up the phone and called the secretary outside his door. "Is Ms. Langston in her office?"

"No, sir. She went out to lunch about half an hour ago."

"If she comes in, will you let me know?"

"Certainly, Mr. Crawford."

He replaced the phone. "She hasn't been seen since she left for lunch half an hour ago."

"I don't know why she got so upset," Beth said. "She should be grateful."

Michael sighed. "Receiving can be just as hard as giving. Maybe harder."

"Humph!" Beth crossed her arms over her chest.

"Michael's right, Beth," Melissa said.

"I suspect it's not the first time people have given things to her." Abby's eyes were focused on a painting on the wall. "She's worked hard to be in a po-

sition where she didn't have to take charity anymore.''

"It wasn't charity!" Beth protested.

"I'm not sure Dani understood that." Abby stood
and paced the floor for a minute or two. Then she
stopped and stared at Michael. "What do we do
now?"

"I'll try to talk to her when she comes in."

"All right," Abby agreed. "We'll go back home
and wait."

He escorted the ladies to the main door. After they
walked away, he turned toward his office, but the secretary stopped him.

"Mr. Crawford? Ms. Langston called and said she
got sick suddenly and couldn't come back to the office."

Great. Now what was he going to do? "How did
Ms. Langston sound?" he asked Angie.

"I'm sure I don't—"

"I'm only asking because she knows no one here
and if she needs help, I don't know whom she'd
call."

"Oh! Poor thing. Well, it sounded as if she'd been
crying. But it could be that she has the flu. That stuff
can hit suddenly."

"All right, thanks. I'm going to go check on her.
I'll be back."

He was heading out of the building before Angie
could respond. In the parking lot he noted that Dani's
car was missing. He drove to the apartment unit she'd
entered that morning. Finding her car, he parked beside it.

When he knocked on the door, there was no answer. He put his ear against the door and barely heard some movement. He knocked again. Then he said loudly, "If you don't answer the door, Dani, I'm going to have the manager unlock it. I...I'm afraid you might commit suicide."

The door opened immediately. Dani stuck her head out and looked to the right and left.

"Are you trying to ruin my reputation?" she demanded.

Michael ignored her question. Instead he focused on her swollen eyes and pale face. "You called in sick."

As usual, she gave nothing away. "So?"

"Are you sick?"

"Why would I call in sick if I wasn't?" she replied.

"Maybe because you were upset and didn't want anyone to know."

She said nothing, just stood there gripping the door and staring at him.

He reached out and took her hand. "Dani, do you want to talk about it?" Concern dripped from his voice.

"No."

"Why not?"

"Because it's none of your business."

"I think it is. We're friends, at the least."

Saying nothing, she started to close the door.

Michael quickly inserted his foot and the door banged against his thick-soled shoe.

Dani sighed. "Michael, we hardly know each

other. We are not friends. You owe me nothing." With that she tried to close the door again.

He didn't move. "I promised I'd talk to you. Abby is upset."

Dani looked at him a moment, then released the doorknob and walked away, keeping her back to him. "I'm sorry," she said over her shoulder. "I didn't ask for money."

"Abby knows that, honey. She and her sisters wanted to give you the money because they thought that was what Beulah would want."

She jumped when Michael put his hands on her shoulders. Pulling away, she wiped her eyes and turned to face him. "I turned them down."

"I know."

"Then there's nothing to say."

He stepped closer again. "Yes, there is. Abby doesn't want to lose your friendship."

Dani's eyes began blinking rapidly as she fought back more tears.

"I think it would be best if—I probably won't be in the area much longer, so—"

He didn't give her time to finish her sentence. Not when she spoke of leaving. "Why?"

"I think I need to move on." She tried to nonchalantly wipe her eyes, but Michael caught her hand. Then he caught a tear on his fingertip.

Lifting her chin with a bent finger, he looked at her sincerely. "Crying doesn't make you weak, Dani. It means you care."

"Caring can be a costly thing. I…I like Abby and her sisters. But the only thing we have in common is

Beulah, and I never met her. I don't live the same kind of life or do the same things. There's nothing on which to build a friendship.''

"Come to dinner tonight with me at Abby and Logan's house.''

She turned her face away. ''Absolutely not!''

"It will let Abby know that you don't hate her.''

"Of course I don't hate her!''

"She thinks you do.''

Once again she tried to back away, but he stopped her. ''Let me go, Michael. I'm not going to the ranch again.''

"Please. Just this once. If you don't want to come back, I won't insist, but you need to go tonight, to have closure.''

"Oh, please! I don't need—''

"Abby does. She's tenderhearted. And Logan would appreciate it, too. If you don't, she'll cry. Logan goes crazy when Abby cries.''

She didn't seem to find the humor in his remark. ''I'm sure she wouldn't.''

"I know she would. She liked you from the very beginning. Now she feels responsible for you. That's how older sisters are. Older brothers are that way, too. Believe me, I know, since I have four of them.''

Dani sniffed. Then she said, ''Just Abby, not her sisters? And she won't try again to give me money?''

"Absolutely not. I promise.''

"All right, Michael. I'll come. What time?''

"I'll pick you up after work.'' He pulled her toward him and kissed her cheek.

"But then you'll have to drive back into town to bring me home. There's no need for that."

He ignored her argument and forged ahead. "I'll be here about five-thirty. And, Dani, I appreciate you doing this for Abby and Logan."

Before she could change her mind he took his leave. He thought it was important for Dani to reestablish a relationship with Abby before it became a big embarrassment and a protracted separation. Otherwise he didn't figure Dani would stay in Wichita Falls. She'd leave before she had a chance to establish her career.

And, more important, before he could convince her there was something between them.

Chapter Nine

Dani regretted her agreement almost at once. Several times during the afternoon, she picked up the phone to call Michael and tell him she'd changed her mind.

But she didn't want to cause Abby any stress. She'd been more than kind. Dani couldn't repay that kindness with rudeness. It was just going to be dinner, she reminded herself, with no mention of the difficult subject.

Michael had promised.

She'd realized he was a bigger problem than Abby. He didn't hesitate to kiss her whenever he wanted. Not that she'd protested much. Which, of course, was the biggest problem.

As a child, she'd hidden in the closet late at night when her mother "entertained" her men friends. She'd kept to herself most of her life. What little sexual contact she'd had as an adult hadn't turned out too well.

So tonight would be her last time spent with Michael. That had to be, she lectured herself. Except at the office. She'd have no choice but to see him there—if she stayed.

Her head was spinning with so much to decide. Normally she made her decisions with logic, not emotion. Now, though, she seemed to be an emotional basket case, with tears rolling down her cheeks. She needed to return to her stoic response. But having let the feelings out, she was having trouble reining them in.

What was she going to do?

Her choices disappeared when Michael arrived at her door about fifteen minutes early.

"It's not time yet!" she immediately said.

"I got away a little early. But if you're not ready, I can wait." He came in and sat in the one chair in the room. "Bought any furniture yet?"

"No."

"You don't have a television either?"

"No, I don't." After standing there staring at him, she said, "I'm ready."

"Oh, good." He stood up. "Ellen's cooking chicken fried steak, so I don't want to be late."

In the car, Michael kept the conversation going by talking about work. Though Dani knew he was purposely trying to distract her, he still succeeded. She enjoyed her work.

"No more problems with Cobb?" he asked.

"No. Though he'll probably question me tomorrow about going home early today."

"Tell him you had female problems. He won't question you about that."

She jerked her head to the side to look at him. "Michael! That would be lying!"

"So? Is it his business that you got upset about your family?"

"They're not really my family. There's no blood kin."

"I don't think you understand how the girls feel about Beulah. Logan had to talk long and hard to stop Abby from naming their daughter after her."

A small smile erupted on her face. "That name wouldn't fit her as well. Mirabelle is perfect, because she always reminds me of Tinkerbell."

"True. She's always popping up where you don't expect her." Michael let out a laugh.

"She is certainly cute. But she doesn't leave much spotlight for Scotty."

"Scotty will be just fine. Didn't you notice Sunday that Logan had him on his horse with him? He's a daddy's boy."

"Did your dad do that for you?" she asked, eager to hear more about his wonderful family.

"Yeah. Along with all my brothers." He paused and took his eyes off the road to look at Dani. "Didn't your mother spoil you?"

"No." Her tone of voice didn't invite questions, but Michael asked anyway.

"Maybe she did and you just don't remember?" he suggested.

"No, Michael. I remember just fine. My mother was an alcoholic and a drug addict. She worked as a prostitute until she died of AIDS. She barely even knew I existed.''

Good thing the traffic was light, because he swung around to face her. ''Who took care of you?''

''I don't know who took care of me when I was a baby. When I was old enough to realize things, about three, I think, I took care of myself.''

''That's too young. You must not remember.''

''Fine.'' She stared straight ahead, fuming. She remembered her life all too clearly, thank you very much.

''Dani, talk to me.''

''Why? So you can tell me I'm wrong?''

''I just meant—I can't imagine a three-year-old managing to feed herself. Or wash her clothes.''

''I didn't wash my clothes. Occasionally my mother would wash a load and include mine. By the time I was eight, I was doing all the laundry by myself.''

''Did your mother do the cooking?''

''No.''

''So how did you eat?''

''I hoarded what she brought home. The jar of peanut butter was my favorite. And occasionally she'd buy a box of cereal. When I started school, my life changed. I learned to read, and the world opened up to me.''

''You like to read?''

''It's one of the most important things in the world to me. At school the teachers were so kind to me. One of them who had older children gave me the clothes they'd outgrown. Before that, the other children made fun of me."

"So your mother took you to school?"

"The first day. After that, I walked to school by myself. It wasn't that far. They enrolled me in the breakfast and lunch programs so I got hot meals twice a day. And the library…" She smiled at the memory. "The library was a miracle. The librarian and I became quite friendly."

An uneasy silence fell upon the car. Suddenly Dani wished she hadn't told him so much. Things she'd never told anyone before.

Michael was the first to speak. "If it wasn't your mother who taught you to cook, how did you learn?"

"The chef at the café I worked in. I thought I told you."

"Maybe I forgot. How old were you?"

"Fourteen."

"I thought you had to be sixteen to work outside the family."

"Joseph figured I'd do better imitating him rather than my mother." She thought fondly of the man till this very day. He was and always would be her friend.

"Did you lock your bedroom door when your mother…entertained?"

"We only had one bedroom. I slept in the closet. She didn't remember I was there."

Dani had a clear mental picture of herself as a frightened child, huddling in the closet, afraid to make a sound. She thought she'd break down and cry as the memories assailed her.

Michael took a hand off the wheel and grabbed one

of hers. "I'm sorry, Dani. I had no idea how bad it was for you."

If he only knew, she thought.

"Let's not talk about it anymore, Michael. The past is better left in the past."

And the future? asked a small voice inside her.

With Michael and the Kennedy clan, she could only take it one day at a time.

Michael parked his car beside the manager's house. "We've got some time before dinner. Want to come in?"

"No, thank you," she said, avoiding his gaze.

"Why?"

"Because you tend to get too friendly if we're alone."

"You mean the kisses? What if I promise not to? We could…talk some more."

"I think we've done enough talking for one day," she said and got out of the car.

Michael sort of agreed. What he'd learned already made him feel guilty for his own childhood. If he heard much more, he probably wouldn't be able to sleep tonight.

Dani started walking toward Abby's house. "If I'm early, I can help Ellen. It's not easy feeding so many people."

Before they reached the steps, Ellen stepped onto the porch, all smiles. "Mercy, child, come in. Seems like forever since I've seen you." She hugged Dani close.

"Ellen, it's only been a few days. I thought you'd be happy to have fewer mouths to feed."

"No, child, we've missed you."

Michael could detect a faint smile light up Dani's blue eyes.

"What can I do to help?" she asked. "Have you made the biscuits yet?"

"Nope. And Floyd says I haven't quite got it right, so I'll leave the biscuit making to the expert," Ellen said with a big grin, drawing Dani to the kitchen counter.

Michael went through the kitchen to Abby's office, knowing Dani would be occupied and entertained by Ellen. He knocked on the door, and as he'd expected, Abby answered.

"Is she here?" Abby asked eagerly when he entered.

"Yes, she is. Abby, did you realize how hard her life was?"

"Well, it can't have been a picnic to put herself through school, like she did. I doubt that her mother helped much."

"She said her mother was an alcoholic and drug addict, and made her money as a prostitute. She said from the time she could remember, she took care of herself."

"Oh, my. Beulah would've taken her in, if she'd known."

"Well, someone should've helped Dani. My life seems so easy compared to hers. I don't think I've ever gone hungry in my life."

"Where is she now?"

"Making biscuits in the kitchen with Ellen."

"Good, Ellen has been worrying about her."

Ellen cut right to the chase.

"I wish you'd come back here to live, Dani. It's not safe in the city."

Dani laughed. "Safety is a state of mind. Bad things can happen anywhere."

"That's probably true." Ellen shrugged. "Is your work going well? You know, it's important to have work you like."

"Work is fine. The two cases I'm working on are for women who've been taken advantage of. So I'm very interested."

"What happened to them?"

Dani launched into a general description of the two cases, keeping Ellen highly entertained. Afterward, Ellen sent her out to ring the dinner bell. Dani liked that tradition. Maybe because it meant you wouldn't be eating alone.

Mirabelle and her father came out of the barn together. When the little girl saw Dani on the back porch, she waved and began to run.

Dani admired Mirabelle's exuberance. She prayed the child would continue to have a happy life. Stepping down from the porch, she went to meet her.

"Dani! You came!" Mirabelle grabbed her hand and tugged her toward the barn. "Come see. Come see."

"What do I need to see? Ellen has dinner ready."

"Hi, Dani," Logan said. "Mirabelle, you can show

Dani the baby colt after dinner.'' He looked at Dani.
''One of our mares gave birth today.''

''Oh, I'd love to see the baby. But we'd better go
after dinner,'' she told Mirabelle.

''Okay, but *I* get to show you, okay?''

''If it's okay with your daddy, that would be
great.''

Immediately, Mirabelle spun around and ran to the
house, yelling over her shoulder, ''I'm going to tell
Mommy.''

Logan sighed. ''I wish I still had that kind of energy!''

''Me, too. But I think Mirabelle got an extra dash
of it when she was born.''

''Probably. She sure came out in a hurry. Impatient
to take on the world.''

''I bet Abby was glad. I've heard long labor isn't
much fun.''

''No, I guess not. So, how's your week been?''

''Fine. Thanks to Michael, I'm actually working on
some cases. It's just what I wanted.''

''Good for you. Did you find a safe place to live?''

''Yes. The first place I stayed wasn't safe, so I
moved again.''

''Leaving your money behind each time?''

Dani smiled. ''This time it was only a week's
worth.''

''You know I'm not going to cash that check, don't
you?''

Dani nodded. ''But you have the right to.''

''Dani, Michael isn't paying any rent, either. I offered to let you pay so you'd be comfortable staying

here, not because I needed the money. I don't come from poor people but I do understand about pride.''

She smiled at Logan. Like his wife, he was exceptionally kind. ''Thank you.''

''Do you even know how much money the girls were trying to give you?'' Logan asked.

''No, but—''

''Five million,'' Logan said, staring at Dani. ''You should be rich, too. Beulah certainly was.''

What did she just hear? Five million? That was more money than she expected to see in two lifetimes. She was so shocked she was speechless. Logan led her into the kitchen.

Abby smiled and made a move to hug her, then stopped. ''Is something wrong?''

''I just told her how much money she'd turned down,'' Logan said with a grin.

''But we promised we wouldn't—'' Abby turned to Dani. ''I'm sorry, Dani. I told Logan he wasn't supposed to talk about that.''

Dani found her voice. ''It's all right. Are we ready to eat?''

Ellen answered that question. ''We surely are. Everyone sit down.''

Dani found Michael beside her at the table as she had the first time she'd eaten there. Conversation was general until Mirabelle remembered to tell her mother about the new arrival in the barn.

''Mommy, there's a baby colt in the barn. Daddy showed me!''

''Ah. Naomi had her baby?'' Abby asked her husband.

"Yep, and he's a beauty."

"After dinner, we can go see him," Abby told her daughter. "Even Scotty might like to see him."

"Me!" Scotty crowed, obviously recognizing his name.

Everyone laughed at his response and Dani felt some of her tension ease away. She'd felt so much a part of the family from the first time she'd met them. She didn't know why, since she'd never felt that emotion before.

Could it be because this was her grandmother's home? She didn't think so. She wasn't a person who placed importance on material things.

"Don't forget to eat," Michael whispered, breaking her out of her reverie.

She turned to him. "What?"

He nodded to her plate. "You haven't eaten anything."

She automatically began eating. She'd been so lost in her thoughts, she'd forgotten the meal.

"Does everything taste all right?" Ellen asked, anxiously looking Dani's way.

"Of course it does, Ellen," Dani assured her. "I've missed your good cooking."

"I still have that spare bedroom," Michael said with a grin, as if he knew what her answer would be.

She wanted to make sure he knew it. "No, thank you."

"Probably just as well," he murmured.

Dani looked at him sharply.

Abby protested at once. "Michael! That's rude!"

Michael shook his head, grinning. "No, it's self-preservation. When I know Dani's that close, I can't get to sleep. That makes me grumpy the next day.''

Logan said nothing, but Dani noticed he gave his brother a sympathetic grin.

''Shame on you, Michael,'' Abby said in exasperation. ''That's not Dani's fault.''

All three of the men chuckled and Dani could feel her cheeks turn red.

Ellen changed the subject. ''Why don't you all go look at the colt while I clear the table? Then you can come back for dessert.''

''I'll stay and help you,'' Dani said at once, grabbing some plates.

Floyd spoke up. ''I've seen the colt. I'll help Ellen. You go see the baby.''

Abby nodded and handed him the dishes. ''Thank you, Floyd.''

As Dani followed everyone to the barn, Scotty rode on his daddy's shoulders, his little hands buried in his daddy's dark hair.

It occurred to Dani that she wanted to marry someone who had experienced a good childhood. She might need some guidance on what mothers should do.

She definitely didn't want any child of hers to have a childhood like hers.

As if reading her thoughts, Abby said quietly, ''Michael was telling me your childhood was…difficult.''

Dani shrugged her shoulders. ''Yes.''

''If Beulah had known, she would've rescued you.''

''My mother said she told Beulah she was pregnant

when she came to see her. But Beulah wanted nothing to do with her. Besides, according to my mother, Beulah had nothing to spare."

Abby chuckled. "That's what we thought, too. She used us as cowboys on the ranch. We thought she couldn't afford to hire real help. But as hard as we worked, she was beside us every minute."

"She must've been tough."

"She was. She was also rich. She'd had oil wells on the ranch, and for almost twenty years they'd pumped oil continuously. Beulah saved all that money. We were shocked when, after she died, her lawyer told us what we'd inherited."

"I guess it was a shock," Dani admitted.

After a cautious look at Dani, Abby added, "That's why we thought you should have some of the riches Beulah left us."

"I don't think she would think that was a good idea. My mother wasn't exactly the kind of person Beulah would have liked."

"I would guess you're right, and that's why she sent her on her way. But she would never have left a child to her care. I'd guess Beulah didn't believe your mother was pregnant."

"I don't blame Beulah."

"I'm glad," Abby said softly.

Some noise drew both of them in the direction of the house and they saw Floyd running toward them.

"Something's wrong!" Abby said at once. "Logan!" she called. He and Michael had gone ahead of the ladies, the children in tow.

Logan turned around. "What is it, Abby?"

"Floyd's running down here," she said as she turned back to the house.

"Michael and I will bring the children to the house. Go ahead," Dani said. She moved toward Michael, who was holding Scotty. Mirabelle had climbed up on the gate to the stable.

"Where's Mommy and Daddy going?" the child asked.

"They need to go talk to Ellen. We'll catch up with them in a minute," Dani said calmly.

Michael slipped his arm around her. "Are you okay?"

"Yes. Where is the colt, Mirabelle? Show me!"

The little girl was easily distracted. She pointed out the colt in the stable with his mother. "I'm bigger than he is!" she bragged.

"I think you are. Shall we go back now and have dessert?" Dani asked even as she took Mirabelle's hand and turned her toward the house. She nodded at Michael. "You'll carry Scotty, won't you?"

"Sure. Hold on, Scotty!" he said as he scooped up the boy.

As they walked, they heard a siren that grew louder each minute.

Michael frowned. "Is that siren coming here?"

Before Dani could speculate, they both saw an ambulance coming down the driveway.

"You take Scotty," Michael said, handing the toddler into Dani's arms. Then he scooped Mirabelle into his and started jogging to the house. "We need to find out who's hurt."

Chapter Ten

Ellen had fallen.

Floyd had spilled some water on the floor, and though he'd warned Ellen as he went for the mop, she'd slipped and fallen on her left hip. For the first time Dani didn't see the warm smile that was a constant feature on Ellen's face. Now it was contorted by intense pain. Luckily Floyd had had the mind to call for an ambulance before he came for Abby and Logan.

Logan tried to comfort Floyd while the ambulance technicians put Ellen on a stretcher.

"I've got to go with her!" Floyd insisted as they moved her to the ambulance.

"Sir, you'll need to follow in your own vehicle. There's not enough room for other passengers," the technician said.

Logan offered to drive him, and Abby moved next to her husband.

"I'm coming, too, if— Dani, I'm sorry to ask, but could you stay with the kids? I don't know when we'll be back."

"Of course I'll stay," Dani answered without hesitation. It was the least she could do for these people. "With Mirabelle to tell me what to do, we'll be fine." She reached down to hug the little girl who nodded her agreement.

"I'll stay and help her," Michael said.

"Thank you both so much." Abby kissed her two children and headed for Logan's truck. "Oh! Dani, can you call Melissa and Beth? I haven't told them."

"Yes, I'll call them. Don't worry about anything. Just take care of Ellen," Dani returned.

Inside the house she could hear the phone ringing. When she reached it, she said a breathless greeting. It was Melissa. She and Rob had heard the ambulance and were worried. Dani explained the situation, then ended with "Michael and I are taking care of the kids."

"Oh, good," Melissa said. "I think I'll call Beth and we'll go to the hospital, too."

"Do you want us to take care of your children, too?" Dani asked, frantically trying to remember just how many children were in Melissa's house. She had a baby, and two little girls she and Rob had adopted. Then they had a family of three children they'd adopted. And Dani thought she remembered several other foster children. And of course Rob's daughter. But she was too upset to count all of them.

"No, I'll leave Rob home with the kids. But thank you for asking. And thanks for pitching in."

"It's not a problem," Dani replied before she hung up the phone. While she felt confident about caring for Mirabelle and Scotty, she wouldn't have known what to do with all of Melissa's children. But she admired Melissa's big heart and willingness to take in families where the adults were gone. She managed to keep the siblings together, just as Beulah had done for them.

When she turned around, Michael had both children at the table with bowls of Ellen's famous peach cobbler topped with ice cream. "That was Melissa. She's going to the hospital, too."

"She doesn't need us to take care of her herd of children, does she?"

"No, Rob is going to stay with them."

Michael let out an exaggerated sigh. "He's a better man than I."

"Me, too. I offered, but I was wondering how we would manage."

He pulled out a chair by Mirabelle. "Sit down. I've fixed you cobbler and ice cream, too. You're going to need the sugar rush for energy," he said as she started to object.

"It's good," Mirabelle told her as she followed Michael's orders.

When Dani took a spoonful from the bowl Michael slid in front of her, she agreed. "Oh my, Mirabelle, you're right. It's very good."

Michael brought his own bowl to the table. "After we finish our dessert, we'll need to do the dishes. Can you play with Scotty while we clean up?" he asked Mirabelle.

"I guess so," she said, showing less enthusiasm for the chore than she had her cobbler.

"That would be a great help for your mommy," Dani told her.

"Mommy's not here," Mirabelle informed her.

"I know. She's helping Ellen now, and she would want us to do what we can to make things better."

Mirabelle looked at Dani, her round eyes assessing and observing. "Are you sure?"

"Very sure. And it will keep us from worrying about Ellen if we stay busy."

"When will Ellen be home? She promised to make me a Mickey Mouse cake."

"For your birthday?" Dani asked.

"No. Just 'cause I like them."

"Well, it may be a while. She may be in the hospital for a few days."

Dani regretted those words as Mirabelle's eyes filled with tears. "I don't want Ellen to go away!"

"She'll be back, sweetie," Michael promised. "Now, eat up. You don't want to have to go to bed without your dessert."

"Daddy always reads us a story, Uncle Mike. Are you going to read to us?"

"Sure. A short book." He gave the child a shrewd look. "I know about you picking out the long books."

Mirabelle giggled, relieving Dani's concern. "Okay, Uncle Mike, I'll pick a short book."

"Good girl," Michael said, kissing her cheek.

He and Dani cleaned the table, then went up to bathe the kids. She was amazed that Mirabelle could handle her own bath and brush her teeth. All Dani had to do was comb her hair for her. Then she went back to check on Scotty. She found Michael as wet as the little boy, both of them enjoying the bath.

"So now I have to mop the bathroom, too?" she whined, pretending to be upset.

"No, I'll do it after I read their story," Michael promised.

She laughed softly. "I was just teasing. I'm glad he's happy."

"Scotty's always happy," Michael said.

Almost at once, Scotty contradicted his uncle. His lips turned down in a pout and his eyes got watery. "Mama?" he said, looking past Dani.

Michael grabbed a towel and started rubbing Scotty dry.

"Let me do that while you go put on dry clothes," Dani said. She finished drying Scotty and then dressed him in his pajamas, adding a kiss or two to his chubby cheeks.

"Mama?" Scotty asked again.

Dani hugged him to her. "Mommy will be back soon. Let's go find Mirabelle and get ready for your story."

By the time she had both children on Mirabelle's bed, resting on a pile of pillows and a blanket over them, Michael reappeared. He crawled in between them on the bed, putting an arm around each of them. Then he opened the book and began reading, both children intent on the pictures and the sound of his voice.

Dani stood at the door, watching the enactment of

scenes she'd only read about. She'd never personally experienced that nighttime ritual nor had she seen anyone else do so.

But here was the real thing. Each child with a loving arm around him and her, holding them close, and a patient adult reading a story with enthusiasm.

Overcome with emotion, she slipped away. She wiped down the bathroom after Scotty's splashathon before returning to the kitchen. By the time she heard Michael's footsteps on the stairs, she was finishing up by wiping down the stove.

"Wow! You've done a good job in here. I figured you'd only be halfway through," Michael said as he took in the spotlessly clean kitchen. "You swept up, too?"

"Yes, of course."

"You're good!"

"I've had a lot of practice," she said, thinking about the nights she'd cleaned the diner where she'd worked, not to mention her home.

"Thanks for everything, Dani." He stepped closer to her. "But there's still one more thing you need to do."

Dani gave him an inquisitive look.

"You need to give out a good-night kiss."

Suddenly nervous, she backed up a step, till Michael explained. "To Mirabelle. She's waiting on you."

Michael smiled as he stood alone in the kitchen, listening to Dani's footsteps hurrying to the little girl's room. She'd practically fled from the room a moment ago, no doubt thinking it was he who wanted the good-night kiss. He'd seen her eyes flare when he approached her.

He'd also seen her face as she'd watched him reading to the two children. It had been a combination of delight and longing. He was sure no one had read her a bedtime story as a child.

The urge to put his arms around her and hold her close forever was growing stronger every day. But he'd learned that Dani didn't do things on impulse. He had to take his time.

When she came back down a few minutes later, a smile on her full pink lips, she looked so beautiful, so enticing that he forgot his vow. He wrapped his arms around her and claimed the good-night kiss he'd teased her about.

The ringing phone saved her from a more prolonged kiss he would have wished to share.

Clearing his throat, Michael answered it. "Hello? Oh, Logan, how's Ellen?"

"She's got some painkillers, so she's doing fine. Floyd is still upset, though. Listen, we're going to stay here tonight so we can see her in the morning at six, before she goes into surgery. If you two can hold the fort that long, I'll be back by seven-thirty. That way you can get to work on time."

"Are you sure?" Michael asked. "I can take off—"

"No, that's not necessary. I think all three girls are going to stay here at least until tomorrow evening. Then things should be back to normal after that. We really appreciate you two pitching in."

"Hell, Logan, we're family. Of course we pitched in."

"Tell Dani how much we appreciate it, too."

"Will do."

When he'd hung up the phone he passed on Logan's praise.

"He thinks everything will be back to normal after tomorrow?" Dani said, worry creasing her brow. "But who's going to do the cooking and cleaning?"

With a sigh, Michael confessed, "I don't know. Maybe Mom will come down."

"That would be too hard on your family." After a moment of silence, she said, "I think I should move back in. I can do the cooking, and do laundry at night."

"Move again? But you just rented an apartment for six months."

"That doesn't matter in an emergency. After things settle down, I'll return to my apartment."

"All right, if you think you can handle it."

"Of course I can. Because I'll have help." She probed his chest with her index finger. "You."

"Hey! I didn't volunteer," Michael teased.

She smiled at him. "I'd better go gather up the dirty clothes and get a head start."

As she started out of the kitchen, Michael murmured to himself, "Looks like you'll have no problem managing to be a wife and mother and a lawyer, too."

Dani stopped in the doorway and turned. "Hey, I heard that. You'd better watch what you say." She put her hands on her hips. "All these cozy kisses and remarks about marriage. You'd pass out if I ever took you up on those hints.''

He laughed. "Try me!"

She seemed to back down. "No. I'm not ready to marry and have a family. In fact, I'm not sure I'll ever want that, because I don't know how it works. Besides, I need to establish my career before I let something like that change my life.''

Michael stood there as she hurried up the stairs. He didn't like hearing his own excuse for not marrying on her lips. She was a woman. She was supposed to have a ticking clock that would push her into marriage.

He shook his head. He may have decided Dani would make a good wife, but it was clear he was a long way from convincing her.

Dani spent the night in the spare bedroom with her door open so she could hear the children if they had a bad dream. She'd set the alarm for an early start. After dressing in her same clothes the next morning, she shifted the load of clothes into the dryer, then headed to the kitchen to start breakfast. As a treat for the kids she made pancake batter and put it in the refrigerator until breakfast time. By then, the coffee was ready and she sat down for a few minutes with a cup.

Michael came in at six-thirty and found her there.

"What? You're not busy?" he teased.

"Not right now. I thought I'd fix breakfast for seven. Isn't that when the kids usually eat?"

"Yeah. Will you have time to dress if we leave

here at seven-thirty?'' He was already showered and in the fresh suit he'd run home for last night.

Dani nodded. ''It doesn't take me long.''

He poured himself a cup of coffee. ''And then we'll go back to your apartment after lunch and pack up your belongings?''

''Well, I've been thinking about that. Maybe it's best if I wait and ask Abby and Logan if they want me to stay. They may not think that's necessary.''

Michael smiled and shook his head.

''What?''

''Abby's not that much of a cook. She can do it, but not like Ellen. And they're going to be short-handed on the ranch with Floyd staying with Ellen. Of course they'll want you to stay.''

''I'll ask first.'' When they heard the ding of the dryer, she took a last sip of her cup of coffee and headed for the stairs.

Michael set his cup down and followed her. In ten minutes they had the clothes folded and taken to each of the bedrooms. Scotty woke up as Michael was putting away his clothes.

''Daddy?'' the little boy called, rubbing his eyes.

''No, Scotty, it's Uncle Michael. Daddy will be here in a few minutes. Ready to get dressed?''

The little boy nodded and slid out of his toddler bed to the floor. Then he held his arms up for Michael to pick him up. The warm little body snuggling up to him brought a sweet feeling. ''All right, little guy.''

Ten minutes later, he and the little boy reached the kitchen, with Scotty all dressed and wide awake. Dani was already in the kitchen and immediately put a small glass of orange juice in front of Scotty.

"Good morning, Scotty. Are you hungry?"

"Hungry!" Scotty agreed.

Dani had a pan of bacon and a pancake griddle on the stove. She immediately poured out six pancakes.

"Where's Mirabelle?" Michael asked. "Does she need help?"

"She said she didn't. Would you check on her?"

"Sure." He ran into Mirabelle on the stairs, fully dressed in matching pants and shirt. "You look very nice this morning."

"Thank you," the little girl said politely, pleasing Michael. She didn't always remember the niceties. "Dani said Daddy's coming home this morning."

"Yes, he is. And Dani is making pancakes."

"Oh, goodie!" Mirabelle exclaimed and raced past Michael to the kitchen. That was more her style, so Michael felt everything was okay.

When he got back to the table, pancakes were set at four places and they sat down to eat. Michael couldn't help but think how much they looked like a family—and how much he liked it.

Silence reigned in the kitchen until they all heard a truck.

Mirabelle jumped from her chair and raced out the door. Scotty was slow enough for Michael to catch. The little boy was torn between his father and his pancakes.

When Logan came in the door, carrying Mirabelle, Dani was already making more pancakes. While they browned, she filled a cup of coffee for Logan.

"Wow! What service! And the kids are already dressed. You two worked miracles," Logan said. He put Mirabelle in her chair and then swept up Scotty and gave him a bear hug. "Were you a good boy?"

"Mmm-hmm. 'Cakes!"

"I see. They look good. But, Dani, you don't have to wait on us. You've got to get to work."

"We're leaving in just a minute."

When Logan sat down at the table and started eating, expressing appreciation to Dani, Michael said, "She's got an offer for you you're not going to believe."

"No!" Dani said quickly, causing both men to turn and stare at her.

Michael was surprised. "You changed your mind?"

"What is it, Dani?" Logan asked.

"I'd rather not say until I talk to Abby. It would affect her the most, and she might not want me to— to— Do you mind, Logan?"

"Not at all. That's your choice. But we sure appreciate your pitching in yesterday."

"I've enjoyed it. You have wonderful kids."

Logan smiled and thanked her. "Now you two go on. Get to work. I'll take over here."

It wasn't until they were in the car heading for Dani's apartment that Michael asked her why she hadn't said something to Logan about moving in.

"Because it would force him into an embarrassing position. Besides, it will affect Abby most of all. She should make that decision."

"No one would turn down that offer, honey. Abby would rather have you than some stranger."

Dani didn't say anything else till they reached her apartment and she opened her door. "Thanks. I'll see you at work."

Michael shook his head. "No. I'm waiting for you."

"There's no need. My car is here."

"You may need my car to carry everything back to Abby's. So I'll be coming here after work, anyway. I'll wait right here, but you'd better hurry."

Dani gave him an angry glare, but he ignored her. He was determined to take her to work.

Ten minutes later, she appeared in a slim skirt and jacket and matching navy heels, her hair piled on top of her head and subtle makeup on. He was impressed.

"All that in ten minutes? You look great."

"Thanks." She got in his car without arguing, which relieved him.

They made it to work with five minutes to spare.

Chapter Eleven

Dani didn't know whether to offer to help out. If she wasn't careful, she'd be back where she started, pushing too hard to become a member of the family.

She was able to help, wanted to help, but she didn't want to force herself on anyone. When she got ready to leave that afternoon, she realized she had to wait for Michael. He was in a meeting with his team of lawyers. It amazed her how attuned she was to Michael's coming and going, how easily she accepted him. It frightened her a bit. She was coming to care too much for him.

Dani had decided to go to the ranch and fix dinner. Then, after Abby got home, she'd wait for the opportunity to offer her assistance. She could go get her things afterward. Michael would insist on taking her, no doubt.

He was becoming quite bossy. Protective. She had to admit, she loved it. But still, she thought it was dangerous to come to rely on someone who might not always be around.

"Sorry I ran late," Michael said as he saw her waiting by the secretary's desk.

"It's all right. But I think I should drive my own car to the ranch."

"Of course you should, if you're going to live there," he agreed easily.

She didn't say anything.

Looking at her sharply, Michael said, "You haven't changed your mind, have you?"

"No, *I* haven't, but I don't want to force myself on Abby. She may have worked things out with her sisters."

"And I think you're wrong."

She didn't argue with him. She simply got into his car and let him drive her to her apartment.

"I won't take long," she said as she opened the car door.

"You do intend to pack everything, don't you?" Michael asked, frustration in his voice.

"No. Not when I might not have to."

"And I'm telling you, you do." He got out of the car and followed her.

"Michael, last time I allowed your family to pressure me to move in long before I should have. This time I'll make the decision."

He grunted and folded his arms over his chest on the doorstep of her apartment.

She got the message. He wasn't budging until she did. She suspected stubbornness ran in the Crawford family. "Is Logan stubborn?" she asked.

"Why?"

"I just wondered if it's a family trait," she said as she picked the smaller bag and folded several pieces of clothing to put in it.

"Yeah. But the most stubborn of all is my sister, Lindsay."

"What makes you think that?"

"Her husband says she is."

"But then he hasn't lived with any of you, has he? So he could be wrong."

With that Dani picked up the small suitcase and walked past him. Or tried to. He pulled her into his arms for a brief kiss. Then he took the suitcase away from her. "I'm holding this hostage in my car."

"You don't trust me?"

"I trust you to do what you think is right. But we don't always agree."

She studied him. "You're too smart. That was a good answer."

He grinned and guided her out to their cars.

When Dani got to the ranch, Logan was in the kitchen, standing over a pot of boiling water.

"Hi, guys! Come on in. I'll add a couple more hot dogs."

Dani stared at the mess he'd made in the kitchen without actually cooking anything. "Are—are hot dogs your favorite?"

"Hell—I mean, heck, no!" he said as Mirabelle came into the kitchen. "What do you need, honey?"

"Scotty's hungry," she said before greeting Michael and Dani.

"How do you know Scotty is hungry?" Dani asked.

"He's chewing on the sofa," Mirabelle said without concern.

Logan and Michael both hurried into the living room.

Dani looked at Mirabelle. "Do you like hot dogs?"

Mirabelle shook her head. "But Daddy says that's all he can cook."

"I see." Dani remembered a pasta dish she used to make with sausage links chopped up in it. She supposed hot dogs would work just as well. As she checked the pantry for the other ingredients, the two men came back in, Logan carrying Scotty.

"Is he all right?" Dani asked as she began working on her idea.

Michael laughed. "He's okay, but the sofa has a few teeth marks."

As she chopped the wieners, Logan gave her a confused look. "Uh, what are you doing?" he asked.

Dani stopped at once. "I thought you might prefer a casserole. But I forgot to ask you. I'm so sorry."

Logan looked at Dani and then his brother. "Is she for real?"

The brothers shared a laugh, then Michael said, "Absolutely. Almost too good to be true, eh?"

"Have you heard from Abby?"

Logan thanked Dani for saving their dinner, then gave them an update on Ellen. "The surgery went well, but it looks like Ellen will be out of commission for several months. Floyd, too. He'll take care of her, and the kids, too, but we're going to have to hire a housekeeper. And maybe another cowboy. Especially if Abby tries to do the housekeeping and cooking. I don't know what we'll do.''

Michael raised one eyebrow in Dani's direction. She barely shook her head as she took down two packages of strawberry Jell-O. Then she handed Michael four bananas. ''Slice these, please.''

Logan watched Michael quickly do as she asked. ''Hey, Dani, you've got him trained pretty well.''

''Not really,'' she replied. ''He's just trying to be helpful.'' Then she put Logan to work setting the table.

With all of them working, dinner was on the table in no time, while the dessert thickened in the fridge. When the children were brought in to the table, Mirabelle asked, ''Where's Mommy? Daddy, you said she'd be here for dinner.''

''I hear a car. I bet that's Mommy now. Good thing we set a place for her, huh?'' Logan got up and headed for the door. Michael stopped Mirabelle and Scotty from following.

''Give Mommy a minute with Daddy. Then she'll be in to give you a hug.'' Scotty had no trouble with that order because Dani had filled his plate. He was seldom distracted from eating.

Mirabelle, on the other hand, tugged against Michael's hold, informing him in no uncertain terms to let her go. Dani expected him to give in, but to her surprise, he didn't.

''Mirabelle, if you don't mind me, you'll be in time-out when Mommy comes in. That would be sad.''

She turned a thundercloud of a face on him, but when he didn't relent, she climbed back up in her chair. She crossed her arms across her thin chest and glared at her uncle.

When Abby came in, looking exhausted, Mirabelle jumped down from her chair and greeted her mother. Then she explained how mean Uncle Michael had been.

Abby hugged her daughter and praised her for minding Uncle Mike. A subdued Mirabelle climbed back in her chair.

"Thanks, brother," Logan whispered.

Abby took her normal seat at the dinner table and before she even took a forkful of food, exclaimed, "Logan didn't cook this!"

Logan seemed to take no offense. He looked at Dani and grinned. "No, I didn't. Dani came in and pushed me out of the way. Thank goodness."

"This is wonderful. After eating hospital food, all I could think about was a home-cooked meal. Then I remembered Ellen was in the hospital, not the kitchen."

"Have you figured out what you're going to do?" Michael asked.

"No. I guess we'll advertise for a temporary house-keeper and a temporary cowboy. Whichever we can find first," Abby replied with a long sigh.

Michael turned to Dani. "Now are you going to ask them?"

"I guess I have no choice, thanks to you." Dani looked at Abby. "I was going to offer to you in private so you wouldn't feel trapped, but…"

"Offer what?"

"To take Ellen's place."

"But what about your new job?"

"Well, I couldn't keep everything spotless like Ellen does, but I could cook breakfast and dinner and keep up with the laundry, and still do my job."

"She could do that," Michael interjected, "if she lived here again."

"Well, of course she could—I mean, we'd be so grateful if it wouldn't be too hard on you, Dani," Abby finished.

Dani had seen the relief on her tired face and that was all the answer she needed. "Then I'll be glad to do it."

Logan grinned. "Is this what you two were talking about earlier that you thought we might not like? It's the answer to our prayers. With Floyd to take care of Ellen and the kids, we'll be in great shape."

"Dani, I've been so worried all day. How wonderful of you!" Abby said.

Dani smiled and reached over to clasp Abby's hand. "Now I really feel like I'm family. Do you know how great that is for me?"

"I hope it is," Logan said, "because you're going to work hard the next two months."

"It will be fine." She outlined the plan she'd devised that day, which involved Michael's help.

"You make it sound so simple," Abby said with a sigh. "Melissa and Beth offered to share their housekeepers, but I couldn't shortchange them. Now I won't have to. And I promise I'll help as much as I can."

"Good. We'll all work together."

"'Cause we're family," Abby said, beaming as she hugged Dani.

So Dani moved back into the spare bedroom. Michael offered to share the manager's house again, but she turned him down. She did, however, allow him to drive her back into town to get the rest of her luggage.

While she packed, he talked to the apartment manager about breaking her lease. Since he told the manager he was Dani's lawyer and she was moving because of an emergency, the manager agreed to cancel the lease. Michael told him he could keep the first month's rent for his inconvenience.

He went back to the apartment to see if Dani was ready. "I got you out of your lease," he announced as he picked up her big suitcase.

"What? Why did you do that?"

"Because you're not going to be living here," he said matter-of-factly.

"But I'll only be at the ranch for two months."

"I'm not sure about that. Ellen will be able to do some work, but she'll have to start back easy. Build up her strength. Are you going to abandon her the minute she gets out of bed?"

"Well, of course not, but—"

"No, I didn't think you would."

"But he might not hold the apartment for me when I move back to town."

"True," he said, totally unconcerned.

"Michael! That's my decision."

"When the time comes, if you want to move back to town, I'll help you find something. But this place isn't very special."

He watched Dani slowly look around the apartment. Then she turned to him. "You've never been homeless, have you?"

Again he felt the need to hold her close and promise her she never would be homeless again. But she didn't want his pity, he was sure. And she wouldn't believe his assurances.

"Come on. It's getting late. You've got another early start in the morning."

She followed him down the stairs without a word.

As Michael had said, her days started early. But Michael made it a point to appear in the kitchen shortly after she got up. He set the table, did whatever she asked him to do without complaint.

His brother teased him about becoming domesticated, but Michael pointed out that he was just following in Logan's footsteps.

Work at the D.A.'s office continued on an even keel. Ned Cobb ignored Dani most of the time. However, he invited her to accompany him to a campaign luncheon and give a speech about women's rights. As much as she hated public speaking, she highlighted the D.A.'s office's good reputation on harassment cases. She ended her speech by saying she was the only woman lawyer in the office, but she hoped there would soon be several others.

Ned was obviously taken aback by that comment,

but when the audience greeted her words with applause, Ned ultimately agreed. He had no choice.

When she stepped down from the stage, Michael was waiting for her. "Well done."

"I didn't know you were here!" she exclaimed.

"I wasn't going to miss your first campaign speech. I suspect Ned will be having you perform a lot. People respond to you."

"I hope not."

Michael chuckled as he put his arm around her. "What do you say we blow off this rubber chicken lunch and go eat by ourselves?"

"That's not necessary."

Michael ignored her protest. "We'll go to Sunny's, where you met the girls for lunch. I don't think you ate anything on that trip."

"No, but—"

He leaned over and kissed her. "No argument. You're working so hard, you're losing weight, and you don't have any to spare."

"Nonsense!"

He just kept walking out to the car.

Dani had to admit a lunch she didn't prepare and didn't have to clean up after was a pleasure. It was the first time she'd had a leisurely lunch since she started doing two jobs. Normally she used her lunchtimes to plan meals and shopping lists.

Michael set out to entertain her, telling her stories about his childhood, or stories about cases he'd tried. She asked him what he had in mind long-term.

"I want Ned's job."

"You want to be elected D.A.? Why?"

"Because I think he does a lousy job. The office isn't run well. His attorneys don't work very hard, and he's definitely not a good man. Witness the way he treated you."

"I don't disagree, but getting elected can be difficult."

"Yeah, but I figure I'll get you on my side. Then I'm sure to win!" He grinned at her.

She looked at her watch and reminded him of the time. It wasn't that she wouldn't be on his side. Of course she would...if she were still in Wichita Falls.

But the last time she'd thought that far in advance, she'd hoped to make it three months.

A few days later, even leisurely lunches were out of the picture. The wife of the Wichita Falls mayor shot him when she found him in bed with another woman. Mrs. Kay Stone immediately hired an expensive, well-known defense attorney.

As the only female lawyer in the D.A.'s office, Dani was assigned to the prosecution team. At first, the male attorneys ignored Dani, treating her like the token female they believed her to be. Only Michael had been supportive.

Within two weeks, the town had split. The men thought the wife was a murderer. The women thought the mayor deserved what he got.

Finally, Dani pointed out that if they didn't take a different attitude into court, or get an all-male jury, they were going to lose the case. Michael backed Dani. When one of the other lawyers insinuated he was only doing that because he was sleeping with her, the two men almost came to blows.

Ned stepped into the fray and, much to Dani's surprise, supported her. No doubt because he feared for his job, should they lose the high-profile, media-magnet case.

After Ned left the conference room, all the men turned back to Dani. The most senior attorney, Dick, wanted to know what she thought they could do.

Instead of shrinking back in shyness, Dani took the floor. "You've said Mayor Stone had betrayed her again and again, right? Well, I think we need to focus on why she killed him *this* time. Why did this time make a difference? Why would she have tolerated being betrayed so many times, yet not now?"

Suddenly they looked at her, no longer inattentive. They couldn't answer her question.

Michael agreed. "Dani's right. We need to know what changed. We need to interview her friends, acquaintances. Their children, family members. We can't assume that because she pulled the trigger, she'll be punished."

That afternoon as they drove home from the office, Michael and Dani discussed the case.

"I think you may have just saved Ned's bacon," he said. "His staff has become lazy. Today you stirred them up and gave them a goal in this case."

Dani appreciated the compliment but restrained her enthusiasm. "We'll see. Things don't turn around overnight. Half of those guys can be persuaded to think she's innocent if she smiles at them and shows a little cleavage."

"You're right," Michael agreed with a chuckle, "but that describes the male population. And at least half the jury will be men."

"And the other half women who hated the mayor." She sighed. "This is going to be a hard case to win."

"Maybe we can do it, since you've changed the focus of the staff. Nice job."

"We'll see. Anyway, thanks for supporting me."

Michael took one of her hands in his and held it over the console as he drove. "I'll never go against you, Dani."

She gazed over at him, measuring his words. Michael was a good man, but as she'd learned the hard way, never was a long time.

Dani began to think they were never going to find out what had happened with Mrs. Stone. The D.A.'s team talked to her children and family members, but there wasn't even so much as a hint that she'd planned her husband's murder in advance.

She was interviewing several friends of the late mayor's wife at the country club one afternoon. In a large room with the autumn sun streaming in through the windows, Dani noticed how the three ladies perked up as a buff young man came to take their bar orders. All three flirted with him, even though he was at least twenty years younger than they.

The waiter returned their attention, generously spreading his attention to all of them. When he'd left, one of the ladies, Marie Dempsy, sighed. "Too bad he's already taken."

"Oh? He's married?" Dani asked, thinking she'd hate to be the man's wife.

"Not married. But, well, you know."

"Marie," warned one of her friends in a harsh whisper.

Dani's ears perked up. She let one of the others change the subject, but she made a note to get Marie alone. After several rounds of drinks—Dani had only mineral water—the other two women stood to go and suggested Marie should go also.

But she stayed in her upholstered settee she shared with Dani. "I want another drink. Fred's got a business dinner tonight, so I'm not in a hurry."

"I'll keep you company," Dani offered. While the other women pulled Marie to one side and whispered warnings to her, Dani pulled out her cell phone and gave Michael a call, briefly telling him she would be late.

Marie rejoined her at the settee. She was suddenly in a bad mood.

"Is something wrong?" Dani asked in a sympathetic voice.

"Those two don't think I can keep a secret!" Marie seemed perturbed.

"I'm sure you can," Dani said in a soothing voice. "I want to ask you about that bartender. He's awfully handsome." She followed him around the room with her gaze, trying to appear interested. "Did you say he's married?"

"No, but he's…taken. There are lots of lonely women whose husbands are, you know, busy elsewhere. He played the field for a while, but not now."

Dani felt a little melodramatic when she crossed her hand over her heart. "You mean he fell in love?"

Marie gulped another drink. "I guess so. Anyway, he'll probably marry her if she doesn't have to go to jail. And he promised her she wouldn't."

Dani's heart started to pound. Marie was confirming her suspicions that Mrs. Stone and this waiter were lovers. Feigning nonchalance and being careful to not mention names, Dani said, "How can he promise that?"

"He said—" Marie hiccuped. "He said it's a crime of passion and she'll go free, get his money, and they'll live happily ever after." She gave a big sigh. "We're all jealous."

Dani excused herself but instead of using the rest room, she called the two detectives who were working the case. She told the story Marie Dempsy just told her and asked them to check out the waiter's background, see if he had a record. See what they could get out of him.

After saying good-night to Marie, she hurried back to the office to find Michael waiting for her. "I'm so sorry, Michael, but I may have found out how it went down. And if I'm right, it was premeditated."

He hugged her and gave her a congratulatory kiss. She relaxed against him, exhausted from the tension.

"Okay, let's go home. You deserve to get some rest," he said.

"Home? Oh, no! We're late! Everyone's going to be starving!" All the excitement fell out of her like a descending elevator.

"Don't worry. I ordered a barbecue dinner and got

Logan to pick it up. They've already eaten, but they saved us some. So let's go home and celebrate your good news.''

Dani let Michael put his arm around her and lead her out of the building. She relished his warmth, the feel of his body against hers. They were quite a team, she remarked to herself.

But a team involved respect and trust. No doubt she respected Michael—as a lawyer and as a man. And, she grudgingly admitted, she was coming to trust him.

The thought sent a shiver up her spine.

Was it from excitement—or fear?

Chapter Twelve

Dani's find was the break they needed in the case. It turned out the muscled waiter had a record, and the D.A.'s team was putting together what it considered an airtight case against Mrs. Kay Stone, murderer.

Michael was proud of Dani, but he was growing increasingly concerned. Their days in the office were long, involving working lunches and late nights. When they finally did manage to get home for dinner, there was no time to cook it. Because she felt responsible, Dani cooked ahead and froze some dinners that a tired Abby could heat up when she and Logan came in after tending the ranch.

Michael knew Dani was doing more work at the house than he. Hell, she was doing more work than two or three people. He pitched in and did what he could, when he could. But it wasn't enough.

He was getting frustrated with the demands on her time. Even with both of them living at the Circle K, it was impossible to find time to be together. Finally, after one particularly grueling week, he had had it.

He had a great mind, didn't he? Why not use it to come up with a plan?

It was after six-thirty and Dani was still at the office when she got an e-mail from Michael. "Subject: dinner." Her stomach growled at the mention of the word. It had been a long time since the tuna on whole wheat.

A smile broke out on her face when she opened and read the e-mail.

"Dinner tonight at eight—my place, my treat. Don't be late."

She packed it in immediately and met a bemused Michael out by the secretary's empty desk. Instead of feeling exhausted on their ride home, as she usually did, Dani felt excited. She didn't need Michael to tell her she was on overload and needed some down time. But the fact that he'd prepared a special meal just for the two of them touched her. And the fact that he wanted to spend time alone with her thrilled her.

When she got to her room, she changed into jeans and her favorite sweater and combed her hair. She ran back in and splashed on a little perfume at her wrists and behind her ears. Not that she thought Michael intended anything romantic, she reminded herself.

She walked over to his place, a corduroy jacket over her shoulders, and knocked on the front door. Why was her hand shaking? This was Michael. He was the protective type, she told herself, and he was just trying to help her out.

But when she walked in and saw the table aglow in candlelight, the sweater she'd chosen suddenly felt a bit too warm. Michael had the lights off in the adjoining living room, which gave the dining area a romantic, intimate ambience. He welcomed her and set down in front of her a beautiful plate of aromatic food.

"I hope you don't mind, but I picked this up at that new restaurant in town," he said, suddenly looking sheepish. "I wanted you to have something special. And edible," he added, "so I didn't cook it myself."

His attempt at humor elicited a small laugh from her, but she was growing more nervous by the minute.

"How about some mineral water?" Without waiting for her assent, he poured it in a beautiful fluted glass that he no doubt hadn't owned before tonight.

She cleared her throat before she spoke. "Michael, everything looks beautiful." Lifting her eyes up to his, she continued, "Thank you for doing this for me. But you didn't have to."

"Yeah, I did," he said, reaching across the table to take her hand. "You deserve it. Now eat up."

As they ate, they discussed the case, in spite of the candlelight, and Dani could feel herself relaxing and simply enjoying the food and the company. She loved trying out new theories and angles on Michael.

When they'd had their fill of the delicious dinner, Michael suggested they watch a movie he'd rented. "It's a romantic comedy that some of the guys at work said their wives liked. It'll help you relax. Come on." He led her to the cushy sofa that faced the TV.

After he put in the DVD, he joined her there, sliding his arms around her shoulder.

The movie was probably very good, just as the critics had said. But Dani wouldn't know. She wasn't watching it. Not with the lights down low and Michael pressed against her.

She had to admit she loved the solid strength of him. She loved the smell of him, an outdoorsy scent that was all Michael. She loved the fact that, while he wasn't married, he was a family man. She loved his protective streak. In fact, she loved—

She let out an audible gasp as panic flooded her.

She'd fallen in love with Michael Crawford.

"I...I...need to go home," she stammered as she jumped up from the sofa.

Michael turned to stare at her, a confused look on his face. His utterly handsome face. "Why?"

She couldn't tell him why. Instead she lied. "I need to—to firm up my questions for the witness. We're prepping her tomorrow."

He patted the seat beside him. "Sit back down, Dani, and relax. You went over those questions today."

"But I've forgotten them already." She tapped her head. "I'm getting so forgetful lately." She sighed. "I need to go."

As she turned, Michael's warm voice lured her back. "You don't want to sit with me and watch the movie?"

How she wanted! If he only knew.

"Uh, no. I...I can't." That was telling the truth.

She couldn't stay—not if she didn't want to make a fool of herself by telling him that she loved him.

Before he could stop her, she grabbed her jacket and rushed out of the house.

"Did my date come flying through here?"

Logan and Abby looked up from the kitchen table where they were enjoying coffee and pieces of the cheesecake Michael had shared with them.

So much for the dessert he'd planned, to cap off the special dinner. And so much for the kisses he'd planned, to cap off the special night. Michael groaned.

Abby nodded but gave him a confused look. "She came in a second ago and walked right upstairs."

"What did you do to her?" Logan asked.

"I don't know. We had a good dinner…discussed the murder case, nothing romantic. Then we were watching a movie, and she jumped up from the couch and said she had to go. She grabbed her jacket and ran."

Abby took one last bite of cheesecake. "I'll go talk to her."

After she left, Michael sat in her chair. He couldn't believe how badly the night had gone. All his plans…and the night ended with Dani fleeing.

"You didn't hear any screaming or crying, did you?" he asked Logan.

"Nope. She was just a blur." As he scraped his dessert plate with the fork, he said, "And thanks for the cake, bro. It's the best cheesecake I've ever had."

"Yeah," Michael agreed. Too bad he was eating it with his brother and not Dani.

There was a knock on her door. Then, "Dani? Are you asleep?"

The last thing Dani wanted to do was see anyone. But she couldn't ignore Abby. She opened the door. "No, I'm awake. What's wrong?"

"That's what I wanted to know. Michael said you ran out on him."

"Is he here?" She was almost afraid to ask.

"Yes, downstairs. He's worried about you."

That made her feel better and worse at the same time. But she didn't want to see him. "Well, I think I'll just go on to bed," she said. "It's been a long day."

Abby sat silently. Then she said, "Come on, Dani. We're cousins, at least. And I hope friends. You can do better than that."

"No, I can't."

Abby picked up the phone in Dani's room and dialed Melissa. "We're having a hen party. Call Beth and get over here."

Dani stared at Abby, stunned by what she'd done.

Abby got up and said, "I'm going to get us some cheesecake before the guys eat it all. Wait here."

When Abby returned with her two sisters and four plates, Dani didn't know what to do. She'd never been to a hen party in her life.

As usual Beth cut to the chase. "Who's got the problem?"

Melissa smiled at Dani. "You look like you're in

shock, Dani, so it must be you. You see, we get together when our men give us problems. Is it Michael? Isn't he being good to you?''

''He's being very supportive.''

''But…'' Beth prompted.

Dani shrugged her shoulders. ''I don't know what you mean.''

''Do you want more?'' Abby asked. ''I mean, he's as charming as all get-out, and I know he's been trying to help you with everything. So do you want him to be more…personal?''

Dani's cheeks turned a bright red as her eyes widened in shock. ''Absolutely not. I'm not his type at all.''

''I wasn't Jed's type, either,'' Beth confessed with a wide grin. ''But he couldn't keep his hands off me!''

''You two seem so perfect together,'' Dani said, frowning at Beth.

''He said he didn't know how to be part of a family. But he was wrong. He's the best husband in the world and an unbelievable daddy.''

''I don't know much about being in a family, either,'' Dani confessed in a low voice.

''Don't be ridiculous,'' Abby protested. ''Who but family would run themselves ragged doing for us?''

Melissa reached over and touched Dani's hand. ''Your mother may not have taught you about family, but I think you got Beulah's heart. You're family, Dani. I think we all felt it right from the start. And you've proved it to us.''

Dani burst into tears, so overcome with emotion.

She didn't even care that she was crying in front of people.

All three sisters hugged her, assuring her Beulah would be proud of her. Dani dried her tears and thanked them for their reassurances.

"We're not done," Beth said firmly. "You've got to tell us what Michael did to you."

"Nothing! He did nothing. He was being polite, trying to help me relax. He bought dinner and served it at his house and then we watched a movie. I left."

"Why?" Melissa asked softly.

As if she were compelled to answer Melissa's gentle question, Dani explained, "Because I realized I'd fallen in love with him. Which is ridiculous."

"Why is it ridiculous?" Beth asked as she took another bite of cheesecake.

"His family wouldn't like it."

"His mother asks about you every time I talk to her," Abby said.

"She does?"

"Oh, yes. She was almost as proud of you as Michael is for helping us out."

"He is?" Dani asked hopefully.

"He is."

"But that doesn't mean—" Dani broke off, unable to voice her wishes.

"What do you think he was trying to do tonight?" Abby asked, a bright smile on her lips.

"He worries about me working too hard. He said I need to relax," Dani explained.

"Right. He worries about me and Logan, too, but he doesn't invite us over for a candlelight dinner."

"You've got him, girl," Beth said on a smile. "You've just got to reel him in."

Melissa nodded in agreement. "She's right."

"He's downstairs now wondering what he did wrong," Abby pointed out. "You should let him know or he'll be awake all night worrying."

"Oh, no, I don't want that."

"Good! Come along." Abby jumped up and opened the door. "Hen party's over, ladies. But it won't be your last, Dani. It's an old tradition around here."

When Melissa and Beth got up, Dani stared at them. "You expect me to go downstairs and tell Michael I'm in love with him?"

Abby took her by the shoulders. "If you're Beulah's relation, that's what you'll do. She believed in being straightforward."

"And we're behind you," Beth added. "If Michael's not interested, we'll throw him out."

Dani wasn't sure that last statement made her feel any better, but she squared her shoulders. "I'll tell him why I left his house this evening."

They all trooped down the stairs, Dani bringing up the rear.

"What am I going to do?"

Logan looked at his brother. "About what?"

"Dani, of course."

"She's doing fine. In fact, she's doing great. You have nothing to worry about. She's a great cook and a hard worker."

"Of course she is. But does she love me?"

"Why don't you ask her?"

Michael gave Logan a disgusted look. "I'm trying not to make her run away."

"Don't do that! How would we manage?"

"Well, I'm glad to see you can think about someone other than yourself!"

"Aw, come on, Mike. It's not just that. It seems to me that she's feeling like part of the family now. I think she needs that."

"I know she does. But I don't want to be left out."

"Have you told her that? Did she know what you were doing tonight?"

"I told her she needed some relaxation time."

Logan grinned. "Wow, how romantic!"

"What was I supposed to do? Suggest we get married when Ellen gets well again, so she'll have time for me?"

"No, I don't think that has the right touch, either. A little too self-centered. How about—Uh-oh. They're coming down."

Michael stood as first Abby and then her sisters came into the kitchen. Dani was the last one.

Beth and Melissa put their plates in the sink. Then they stepped over to Michael and kissed his cheek. "Good luck," Beth whispered. Melissa only smiled.

In the meantime, Abby was tugging Logan to his feet. "We're going up to bed now. See you in the morning," she said with a smile as they left the kitchen in the opposite direction.

Suddenly there was only Michael and Dani in the big room.

"What's going on?" Michael asked.

Dani kept her gaze fixed on the table. "I need to tell you something."

"Okay." He tried to keep his voice calm, though he worried what she was about to say.

When Dani sat down, Michael returned to his chair, grateful, because he wasn't sure his knees would hold him if she told him she was leaving.

"It was rude of me to run out tonight without telling you why."

That was a start, Michael thought. "I was worried about you. Did I do something wrong?"

She shook her head.

"What—"

"Do you remember when I didn't want to offer to work for Abby because I didn't know if she really wanted me to do that?"

"Sure, but I told you she'd want you."

"Yes, but...do *you?*"

"Do I what?"

Dani pressed her lips tightly together, to keep from screaming. "Do—do you think of me as your little sister?"

"Hell, no!"

Encouraged, she said, "I don't think of you as a brother, either."

He smiled. "I'm glad. How do you think about me?"

"I think I'm falling in love with you. That's why I ran away. And it's okay if you don't think of me that way. But it startled me because I hadn't realized—I've come to rely on you, to count on you. I hope—"

She never finished that thought. Michael pulled her into his arms and kissed her so passionately, she barely remembered where she was.

When he finally freed her lips, she returned the favor, finding a sense of homecoming in his kiss.

Michael looked into her eyes. "I love you, too, Dani." Emotion was in his voice.

"Are you sure? I don't know about families or children."

"You're a smart lady. You'll catch on." He kissed her again.

"Michael, I don't think we should continue—I mean, you're so persuasive and I don't want to—I promised myself I wouldn't…do anything until I was married. Because of my mother."

"Good. So shall we go to Oklahoma and get married this weekend?"

"That soon?" She thought about it. "That would probably be best. I'm tempted too much."

Michael laughed out loud. "Right. You don't know much about families. Watch this."

He crossed to the staircase. "Abby?"

Immediately, he got an answer. "Yes, Michael? Is everything all right?"

"Can you and Logan come down here?"

"What are you doing?" Dani whispered at his side.

"Giving you your first lesson in family."

Abby and Logan came downstairs.

Michael put his arm around Dani. "Dani and I are in love. We thought we'd drive to Oklahoma and get married this weekend."

Abby let out a whoop and ran to embrace them, as

did Logan. Then Abby said, "Of course you won't run off and get married. We'll have the wedding in our church." She looked at Michael. "Call your mom and tell her now, and then I'll call her in the morning and start coordinating everything. I think an early-December wedding will be perfect. Ellen will be well enough by then to make the wedding cake. Who will you choose as your maid of honor, Dani?"

"Or matron of honor?" Michael added with a wide grin.

"Well, you, of course, Abby, if you would."

"I'd love to," Abby said with a big smile. "I shouldn't be too big then."

That statement brought Michael and Dani to a sudden stop. "Too big?" Dani echoed.

Logan beamed at them. "We hadn't told you, but we're having another baby."

"Oh, that's wonderful!" Dani said as she hugged her soon-to-be sister-in-law.

"Yes, but it's absolutely the last one!" Abby exclaimed.

Logan held out a finger to his wife. "Hey, *I* didn't insist," he said with a grin. "You're the one who couldn't say no."

Abby slipped into Logan's arms and kissed him. "I know. You're such a good persuader."

Dani knew exactly what Abby meant. She stepped closer to Michael, and his arm went around her.

"You see?" Michael whispered. "With family, nothing is simple."

"But it's so wonderful," Dani whispered in return.

"As long as it's you coming down the aisle, I won't be complaining."

When the calendar turned to December, all their friends and acquaintances received an invitation.

Beulah Kennedy's family invites you
to the marriage of Daniele Langston
to the last Crawford bachelor, Michael Crawford,
at The Valley Church at 8:00 p.m. on December 5.
Reception will follow at the Circle K.

Dani stood in a circle of family as she greeted their guests after their wedding. The Crawford family, ever growing, joined the Kennedy family again, making Dani feel doubly blessed.

For a girl who'd fought life alone, Dani had found her happiness in her grandmother and the family she gave her. And she'd found the start of her own family in Michael's eyes...and arms.

The children they would have would be loved and guided through life, learning life's hard lessons through the circle of love the two families had made.

*   *   *   *   *

New York Times bestselling author

ELIZABETH LOWELL

**brings a sensual tale of unrequited love starring
her reader-favorite Mackenzie family!**

FIRE AND RAIN

Carla McQueen had loved Luke Mackenzie for as long as
she could remember. But bitter rejection had caused her to
flee the Rocking M ranch, leaving Luke with only memories
of the girl he secretly loved. Now, years later, Carla has
returned, determined to realize all of her dreams.

*Look for Fire and Rain in May—
wherever books are sold.*

Silhouette ®

Where love comes alive ™

New York Times **bestselling author**

DEBBIE MACOMBER

Lydia Hoffman is the owner of A Good Yarn, a little knitting store
on Blossom Street in Seattle. It represents her dream of a new
beginning, a life free from the cancer that has ravaged her twice.
A life that offers a chance at love.

At one of her classes, Lydia befriends three women, each with her
own guarded reasons for needing to learn how to knit a baby blanket.
Brought together by the age-old craft of knitting, they make unexpected
discoveries—discoveries that lead to love, to friendship and acceptance,
to laughter and dreams. Discoveries only women can share...

The Shop on Blossom Street

"Debbie Macomber's gift for understanding the souls of women—
their relationships, their values, their lives—is at its peak here."
—*BookPage* on *Between Friends*

Available in May 2004 wherever books are sold.

If you enjoyed what you just read,
then we've got an offer you can't resist!

Take 2 bestselling
love stories FREE!
Plus get a FREE surprise gift!

Clip this page and mail it to Silhouette Reader Service

IN U.S.A.
3010 Walden Ave.
P.O. Box 1867
Buffalo, N.Y. 14240-1867

IN CANADA
P.O. Box 609
Fort Erie, Ontario
L2A 5X3

YES! Please send me 2 free Silhouette Romance® novels and my free surprise gift. After receiving them, if I don't wish to receive anymore, I can return the shipping statement marked cancel. If I don't cancel, I will receive 6 brand-new novels every month, before they're available in stores! In the U.S.A., bill me at the bargain price of $21.34 per shipment plus 25¢ shipping and handling per book and applicable sales tax, if any*. In Canada, bill me at the bargain price of $24.68 plus 25¢ shipping and handling per book and applicable taxes**. That's the complete price and a savings of at least 10% off the cover prices—what a great deal! I understand that accepting the 2 free books and gift places me under no obligation ever to buy any books. I can always return a shipment and cancel at any time. Even if I never buy another book from Silhouette, the 2 free books and gift are mine to keep forever.

209 SDN DU9H
309 SDN DU9J

Name	(PLEASE PRINT)	
Address	Apt.#	
City	State/Prov.	Zip/Postal Code

* Terms and prices subject to change without notice. Sales tax applicable in N.Y.
** Canadian residents will be charged applicable provincial taxes and GST.
   All orders subject to approval. Offer limited to one per household and not valid to current Silhouette Romance® subscribers.
   ® are registered trademarks of Harlequin Books S.A., used under license.

SROM03   ©1998 Harlequin Enterprises Limited

SILHOUETTE *Romance*®

COMING NEXT MONTH

#1718 CATTLEMAN'S PRIDE—Diana Palmer
Long, Tall Texans

When taciturn rancher Jordan Powell made it his personal cru-
sade to help his spirited neighbor Libby Collins hold on
to her beloved homestead, everyone in Jacobsville waited
with bated breath for passion to flare between these sparring
partners. Could Libby accomplish what no woman had before
and tame this Long, Tall Texan's restless heart?

#1719 MIDAS'S BRIDE—Myrna Mackenzie
The Brides of Red Rose

Single father Griffin O'Dell decided acquiring a palatial retreat
for him and his son was much better than acquiring a wife. But
the local landscaper, Abby Chesney, was not only making his
home a showplace, she was making trouble! The attractive moth-
er-to-be had already captivated Griffin's young son, and now it
looked as if Griffin was next on the list!

#1720 HER MILLIONAIRE MARINE—Cathie Linz
Men of Honor

Attorney Kate Bradley had always thought Striker Kozlowski
was hotter than a San Antonio summer—even after he joined the
marines and his grandfather disowned him. Now the hardened
soldier was back in town and temporarily running the family oil
business with Kate's help. Striker didn't remember her, but she
had sixty days to become someone he'd never forget....

#1721 DR. CHARMING—Judith McWilliams

Dr. Nick Balfour took one look at Gina Tesserk and realized he'd
found the answer to his prayers. After all, what man wouldn't
want a stunning woman tending his house? Nick hired her to
work as his housekeeper until she was back on her feet. He never
anticipated a few kisses with the passionate beauty would sweep
him off his!

SRCNM0404